The Conviction and Subsequent Life of Savior Neck

CHRISTIAN TEBORDO

SPUYTEN DU
New York C

ISBN 0-9720662-8-4

Library of Congress Cataloging-in-Publication Data

TeBordo, Christian.
The conviction and subsequent life of Savior Neck / Christian Tebordo.
p. cm.
ISBN 0-9720662-8-4
1. City and town life--Fiction. 2. Police--Fiction. I. Title.
PS3620.E435C66 2004
813'.6--dc22 2004004154

• • •

A boy awakes to the smell of death, and for a moment, it is his own, the smell of his own death. But he is not nauseous. The smell of death is not nauseating when it is your own, when the smell of death is radiating from your nostrils. Your own death smells like withered flowers doused in gasoline, or so I am told.

His death does not feel like another's either. Another's death feels like cold rubber on velvet cushions. Another's death makes me envy another, makes me envy the peace of another.

The boy worries that he may cry at his own funeral. If death continues to feel the way that it feels, to smell like withered flowers doused in gasoline, he will certainly cry at his own funeral. He will cry at his own funeral because he is beginning to worry that death is a state of eternal anxiety, eternal life.

The boy lies on his bed, listening to his pulse in his pillow. His pulse is a marathon, a losing race. He must have died of a heart attack. The boy's pulse indicates that he has died of a heart attack. He puts his hand to his heart. His heart has definitely suffered an attack.

There is no rhythm in his chest. The pulse is in the pillow. It must have leaked out when he died. The boy lies in bed, his hand on his chest, in a puddle of his pulse.

His heat is there still, in his chest where his pulse used to be. The boy's heart is still hot from the attack. His hand feels the heat from his heart. His heart feels the heat from his hand. His heart races around his ears through the feathers in his pillow, and his death smells like withered flowers doused in gasoline.

The boy's death is a hoax, but he does not suspect that his death is a hoax; that he is slightly less dead than he suspects. He still hasn't doubted the evidence of his death, the smells and leaky pulses. We have to give him time to figure this one out for himself.

He moves his hand from his heart and places it directly in front of his face. He can feel his breath against his hand. His breath is cold against his hand. His breath against his hand feels like a summer hailstorm. It feels as though his hand is in a hailstorm.

He imagines that he can see through his hand. The boy imagines that he can see the beautiful spring morning outside of the window, beyond his hand. He imagines that it is spring beyond his hand. But his hand is no more or less transparent in death than in life. The boy's hand is not transparent, and he has not forgotten that it is winter.

The boy's imagination is not enough to convince him that it is spring beyond his hand. He sees his hand. His hand is not spring. The boy's hand makes him question his death.

He is not ready to deny that the smell of withered flowers doused in gasoline is the smell of his own death. Even after he is granted a pardon, he will think of it as a divine pardon, the boy will still tremble in the knowledge that the smell is the smell of his own death. Years from now, when he passes a florist's shop on the street, if the flowers inside are withered and doused in gasoline, he will shudder, reminded of his mortality. And sometimes he will douse withered flowers with gasoline and say, "This is the smell of my own death."

But the boy has seen enough movies to know that death is transparent, and his hand is not transparent, and his hand is not spring. He clings to opacity in order to confuse his own death.

He does not say, "I am opaque, therefore I am alive,"

because he does not know opaque. He does not say, "I can not see through my hand, therefore I am alive," because he is not necessarily alive. The boy does not dare to be alive.

Yet death is clearly in the room. The boy smells death. He smells withered flowers doused in gasoline, and his pulse is leaking. The boy smells the smell of his own death, and for a moment, it is his father's, the smell of his father's death.

His father, who has taken to crawling quietly into the boy's bed in the time-stands-stillness of the night, lies next to him, smelling of his own death. The boy rolls over, the better to smell it.

The boy's father is transparent. He can see his father's old blue veins through his father's wrinkled skin. He can see his father's bones through his father's sagging flesh. The boy can almost see the cracked plaster wall through his father's sagging flesh. His father's sagging flesh blends with the cracked plaster wall.

The boy pokes his father's transparent shoulder blade with an opaque finger. His father's shoulder feels like cold rubber. It feels like another's death. There is no pulse in his father's shoulder. The boy's father is dead.

He wonders what to do with his dead father. He wonders whether or not he should cover his father's sagging cold-rubber flesh. He pokes his father's transparent shoulder blade with an opaque finger, again and again, savoring the cold rubber of another's death, smelling the smell of his own.

When finally the boy begins to consider, with the gravity called for by the situation, what to do about his dead father, though he has not stopped poking his father's transparent shoulder blade, he is startled by an abrupt movement.

"What?" mumbles his dead father.

Even the dead mumble when they are awakened.

The boy does not answer his dead father. He stops poking his dead father in the shoulder, but he does not answer.

His father does not require an answer. He steals the blanket from his son, covering his own sagging flesh, warming his own cold-rubber flesh.

In his shock, the shock of seeing his dead father move abruptly, of hearing his dead father speak, the boy contemplates the prospect of perpetually sharing a bed with his dead father, at least until he is old enough to move out. The boy shakes this thought from his head, tells himself that everything will be okay.

"Everything will be okay," he says aloud, to himself.

The boy's father sniffs sharply several times. His father smells his own death too. "Did you shit yourself?" he asks.

His father asks him if the smell of withered flowers doused in gasoline, the smell of his own death, is the smell of shit. The boy does not answer. "Did I shit myself?" his father asks, moving his hand to check.

The boy tumbles out of bed and falls to the floor. He falls to the floor and lies motionless. His father's death becomes his own.

The alarm clock rings. The rug jumps beneath the boy. His reflexes have gone the way of his pulse, have leaked out of his body and into the carpet. His pulse is still racing through the bed. The smell of his own death, of withered flowers doused in gasoline, is stronger on the floor.

"Wake up," his father says.

He is awake. And dead. His father is alive and in bed. He hears his father from the doorway. His hearing has leaked from his body and hovers in the doorway.

"Get up," his father says. "Go to school."

The boy does not get up yet. He does not get up and go to school yet. He considers having his father call him in dead.

"My son will not be in today as he has awakened to the smell of withered flowers doused in gasoline. His pulse is in the bed, his reflexes are in the carpet, and his hearing is in the doorway. In short, my son is feeling dead."

He wonders how the administration will react. He wonders what his classmates will think. He imagines his friend speechless, for the first time ever, with sobs; his teacher pale and trembling as the principal leaves the room.

Most of all, he sees one particular girl, eyes moist, lost in a daydream about the future they could have had together had she ever noticed him, and of course, if he had not died. In his daydream of her daydream, they are on a sofa in their lincoln-log cabin, his father already asleep in their bed. She places his hand on her tiny breast, over her blouse, in his daydream of her daydream. In his daydream of her daydream, the parlor smells of fresh flowers.

The carpet weeps beneath him. The floor quakes with the awareness that he will never fondle the girl in their lincoln-log cabin. She will surely forget him long before she is fondled by another man in her lincoln-log cabin. If she remembers to remember him in the first place. The carpet weeps audibly. The boy hears the carpet weeping in the doorway.

His father weeps as well. The boy hears his father. He is crying in bed, crying from the doorway. The boy is not surprised. His father begins each day with a good cry. The boy tells himself that everything will be okay.

"Everything will be okay," he says aloud to himself.

"Nothing," his father hiccups, "will be okay."

"Everything will be okay," the boy whispers. He chants, "Everything will be okay."

The boy stands up. He is going to go to school to see the spectacle that his death creates. He must be present at the announcement of his own death. Perhaps he will announce it himself.

In the bathroom, the boy examines his body in the mirror. The neon sign in the winter beyond the window casts its blue glow on his pinkish skin. His hair is a tangled mess. He showers to give his classmates a good impression of his death. The boy showers so that no one else will smell his own death.

He leaves his apartment, still chanting. He walks down the stairs chanting, "Everything will be okay."

"Everything will be okay," he says outside.

His father opens the window and glares down at his dead son.

"Nothing is going to be okay," his father yells.

His father's pale, sagging skin steams in the winter morning. He leans out the window to make it very clear that nothing is going to be okay. The neon sign casts its blue glare on him. "The Thirteenth Step," it reads as it blues on him. He is a terrible sight. He is an angry god in the winter morning.

"Everything will be okay," the boy whispers.

The soap fairly covers the smell of withered flowers doused in gasoline, but the boy catches the scent occasionally, when his body moves more quickly than his senses, as when, for instance, he looks both ways before crossing the street.

He is joined by his friend on the way to school. "Wait up," says his friend, running down the stairs to his apartment, late as scheduled.

The boy usually waits. He usually waits beside the steps until his friend runs out late, but this morning he is preoccupied. He does not notice his friend when his friend says to wait up. His friend says to wait up, again and again, but he still has to jog on the slippery sidewalk to catch him.

"Everything will be okay," the boy says.

"I know," says his friend, and begins babbling about something or other.

The boy still does not notice him. His friend does not notice that the boy has not noticed him. The boy chants as his friend babbles.

His friend stops at a corner, still babbling, to look both ways, while the boy walks out into the street. A car brakes to a stop inches from the boy, who fails to notice this as well.

"Goddammit," says the man in the car.

"Everything will be okay," says the boy.

The man in the car is comforted by this. He drives on toward work, assured that everything will be okay. The boy tries to assure himself.

His friend finally takes notice. He stops babbling. He looks both ways and then jogs after the boy.

"Hey," he says.

The boy says, "Everything will be okay."

"Hey," says his friend, shoving the boy's opaque shoulder.

The boy snaps out of his stupor, and turns to face his friend.

"What's with you?" says his friend.

The boy looks about and catches the scent of withered flowers doused in gasoline and smothered in soap. He wonders whether he should tell his friend that he is dead now, or wait until the announcement. "I'm dead," he says.

"What'd you do this time?" says his friend. "Did your father find out about the..." He begins babbling again. He enjoys babbling about other people's business as much as he enjoys babbling about his own. A chance to babble about other people's business is a chance to babble about his own. "...We got our asses kicked for that one," he seems to conclude. "But then..."

His friend babbles. The boy does not chant. They walk toward the school.

"...you grounded?" says his friend.

The boy looks both ways before crossing the street.

"No," says the boy, "I'm dead. I woke up this morning to the smell of my own death."

"You're too young to be dead," says his friend.

The boy does not answer him directly. His friend barely notices that he is being contradicted.

"I awoke to the smell of withered flowers doused in gasoline. My pulse is in my bed, my reflexes are in the carpet, and my hearing is in the doorway. In short, I am a dead man."

"A dead boy," says his friend.

"A dead boy," says the boy.

They finish their walk in silence. There is surprisingly little noise from the city.

His friend stares ahead, now and then forgetting to look both ways before crossing the street. The boy looks at the ground saying everything will be okay. He does not say it aloud, but he tells himself that everything will be okay.

At the main entrance to the school, his friend turns toward the boy. He looks at the boy in profile. He opens his mouth. He closes his mouth. He opens his mouth and says to the boy, "Maybe you should keep quiet about this whole being-dead thing."

They walk through the doors.

In class, the boy sits quietly at his own desk. He waits for the perfect moment to announce his own death. The moment does not seem to come.

Sometimes he ponders his death. In the classroom, the boy ponders his own death. As the day wears on, the soap wears off, and he smells his own death more frequently, particularly at recess.

At recess, the class slides around on a big puddle of ice in the parking lot. The boy stands alone on the puddle of ice.

He watches the girl. The girl slides on the ice with her friends.

A group of kids slide out of control and hit the boy. They all topple over one another. The sudden movement brings the smell to the boy's nostrils. One of the kids says, "Somebody smells like shit."

The boy sits where he has fallen, alone on the large puddle of ice. He sits alone and watches the girl.

The teacher walks about the classroom. She walks about the classroom asking and answering questions. She stops behind the boy.

"Can you tell the class...?" says the teacher.

He is thinking about his own death, and about the girl's reaction to his own death. The teacher notices his distraction. She leans down to whisper to him about his distraction and the potential consequences of his distraction. When the teacher leans down to whisper to the boy, she catches a breath of his own death.

The boy is startled when he smells her. She smells of bottled flowers. She smells like the lincoln-log cabin in his daydream of the girl's daydream. He turns to find his teacher squatting beside him.

"Ma'am?" he says.

"You're not feeling well," she says. "Maybe you should go to the nurse."

The boy is surprised to learn that he is not feeling well. Apart from being dead, he has nothing to complain about. But he doesn't argue with authority figures. He leaves the classroom.

"So," says the nurse, "what's the problem?"

Being dead is a problem insofar as he will never fondle the girl in their lincoln-log cabin. Otherwise, being dead has been much like being alive, and therefore is no more a problem than life itself.

"I awoke to the smell of withered flowers doused in gasoline. My pulse is in my bed, my reflexes are in the carpet, and my hearing is in the doorway. In short, I am feeling dead."

The nurse's reaction confirms that being dead is indeed a problem, and she prepares to do a battery of tests, with what little equipment the school district has provided her, in order to deny her patient's self-diagnosis.

She takes the boy's wrist in her hand, and looks toward a clock on the wall. She moves her fingers about on his wrist. She takes his other wrist. The boy sees the frustration in her movements.

"I told you," says the boy, "my pulse leaked out of me and into my bed."

"Nonsense," says the nurse, and bends down to put her ear to his heart.

As she bends down to put her ear to his heart, the nurse catches a breath of the boy's death.

Suddenly the nurse panics. She runs around the room ranting, "This boy is dead I've never treated a dead boy I don't know the first thing about death," she says.

"Young man," she says, "you are dead, young man."

"Everything will be okay," says the boy.

The nurse is comforted by this. She stops running about and ranting. She sends him home, assured that everything will be okay. The boy leaves, wishing that he could assure himself.

The boy walks home telling himself that everything will be okay. The smell of his own death has freed itself of the soap, and he breathes it regardless of whether he looks both ways before crossing the street. He looks both ways before crossing the street.

He sees his father through the window of the Thirteenth Step. His father sits on a stool, a drink in front of him, in candid conversation with the bartender. The boy imagines that he can read lips. "Nothing is going to be okay," say his father's lips.

"Everything will be okay," says the boy.

He walks up the stairs and into the apartment. His father has left a note on the door reminding him to dump their garbage in the neighbor's trash can, and that nothing will be okay.

"Everything will be okay," says the boy, and the apartment echoes its agreement, which is comforting.

He lies down and falls asleep.

The boy awakes to the stench of withered flowers doused in gasoline, and for just a bit longer it is the stench of his own death. He awakes to the stench of his own death and a knock at the door. He assumes that his father has forgotten his keys again. He does not bother to groom himself to give whoever is at the door a good impression of his own death, since he assumes that it is his father.

He opens the door to the girl. The girl stands smiling in the hallway. "You look like death warmed over," says the girl, still smiling. She pities boys who look like death warmed over.

"That's because I'm dead," says the boy.

"I know," she says, "Harold told us at lunch."

The two stand in silence for a few moments. The boy has forgotten his manners. The girl invites herself in. She walks over to the couch and sits down. "So I brought your homework," she says.

The boy is awed by her consideration. He moves toward the couch and sits down beside the girl. Perhaps he sits a bit too close to the girl. The girl sniffs the air. She stands abruptly. "You never gave me the grand tour," she says.

"The grand tour of what?" says the boy.

"Of your apartment," she says.

He has never given her the grand tour. She has never been in his apartment. She has never even spoken to him before. They have never made eye contact as far as the boy can remember. The boy is certain he would remember if they had made eye contact.

The boy remains seated, pointing to the kitchen, the bathroom, and his bedroom saying, "That's the kitchen, the bathroom, my bedroom..."

"Your bedroom?" she says, walking toward his bedroom.

He follows her into his bedroom. She stands silently with her back to him. He imagines that she is transparent, that he can see her smiling face from behind her.

But the girl is not dead. She is opaque. He cannot see through her, which is why the boy is startled by the look of disgust on her face when she turns around.

"Did you shit your bed?" she says.

The boy remains standing, just inside his bedroom. He remains where he is as the girl runs past him and out of the apartment.

"That's just the smell of my own death," he is saying as the door slams behind the girl.

The boy leans against the wall. He slides down the wall. He sits on his bedroom floor with his back to the wall.

"Everything is okay," he says to himself.

And everything is okay. This is just the first disappointment in what will be a long series of disappointments.

Death is a long series of disappointments.

POINT A

Discord in thirteen steps

Let us not delude or confuse or amuse ourselves. Yes, Discord, New York, is a rotten shell of abandoned textile factories and tenement housing, but what, I might ask, if only to force a point, does that have to do with fate? The Discord River sometimes oozes its thick brown-green discordancy over the Discordant Falls, but the industry that it used to power produced a fabric of much lower quality, though admittedly of more existential substance, than that of the ancient Greeks.

Let us, just for a moment then, amuse, if not confuse and delude, ourselves. Let us forget that there's a Discord, an actual broken-brick and cracked-concrete setting for an actual story in which fate played no role. Let's abandon Discord like prosperity did, in favor of the Ideal, the Form of an abandoned Discord.

Look at the old mills crumbling around their shattered windows. Beyond them, industrial darkness, a playground for pigeons. See the cobblestone streets, not a result of old-timey flavor but of neglect, the asphalt rinsed away by decades of rock salt trickling along the curbs toward rusty sewer grates. This is a Discord we can all understand, a Discord we've all driven through on our respective routes, a Discord that we've surely seen on television.

If we turn our attention from this most abstract of Discords toward the most abstract of neighborhood bars, we'll find the Thirteenth Step in the middle of a block on Main Street, in the quote-unquote business district. The Thirteenth Step, though, is an actual bar in an actual quote-unquote business district, and we can't climb the steps and pass through its door without descending from this Olympus we've dubbed delusion, confusion, and amusement. The patron fates of the city, speaking poetically.

Motion Demonstrated Through a Preliminary Rant Against Fate

In a sense it was Harold Esquire, Esq. who set it all in motion. Must we admit, must we take it as axiomatic, that Harold Esquire, Esq. set it all in motion? I'm now and then reminded of Diogenes, who, rather than open his mouth (this was before philosophy meant pen-to-paper), walked from point A to point B. I've only heard the story told anecdotally, but I think it's safe to assume that for Diogenes' response to have been effective, the Eleatics would have to have been a bunch of babblers. So I ask you to imagine that I've run on and on, even more than I actually have, because I've already lost track of points A and B. Or else I'm pretending I've lost track of points A and B, if only to deny motion, if only to deny that Harold Esquire, Esq. set it all in motion.

But I won't even bother to deny that Harold Esquire, Esq. was on television—the one on the shelf in the right-hand corner behind the bar—on the night that neither he nor the fates set it all in motion. He was there—on the screen, blurred with static, outlined by snow, and scanned periodically by horizontal lines of color—beside Richie Repetition, the local speedfreak, notorious for petty thievery and assault.

It wasn't the electrical static that made Richie Repetition appear kinetic. Richie Repetition was kinetic. Every nerve in his body was throbbing, starving for the methamphetamines that he couldn't snort in court, or on the courthouse steps.

The courthouse spread its neo-Romanesque self out heavily behind the criminal and the lawyer who had just gotten his case—a case involving an attack on Thomas Didymus, an old-looking young man who spent most of his time beneath a highway overpass inhaling gasoline fumes from a can—dismissed. An overcast sky rested atop the building betraying the fact that, though the word "live" appeared on the lower left corner of the screen, the newscast had been taped much earlier.

Outside of the Thirteenth Step, night had fallen hours before, and the snow had fallen, and continued falling on the night, and the streets of Discord were paved with a cold, dangerous mess. The winter on the sidewalks was staticky-silent, like Richie Repetition.

Harold Esquire, Esq. was anything but silent. He ranted and panted and blathered all over the screen, bumping into Richie Repetition and slamming him in the kinetic head with stray gestures. Richie Repetition took the unintentional punishment, or misdirected congratulations as you might have it, meekly. It was better than doing time in the county correctional facility. Again.

Coincidentally, Harold Esquire, Esq.'s noise couldn't yet be heard in the Thirteenth Step. The volume on the television set was down, as it usually was, to accommodate someone's dreaming a little dream from somewhere within the jukebox. The mumble of the occasional conversation seasoned the room with its blandness. Put any other picture on the television screen, and it could have been any other night at the Thirteenth Step.

Any other night, that is, besides the nights that Richie Repetition appeared on *The Penny Dreadful Show*, and these nights were numerous enough to count as a significant sub of the set nights at the Thirteenth Step. On such nights, as on the particular night that concerns us, someone in the room was bound to mumble, "Richie's on," and Vinnie Domino, the owner and proprietor of the Thirteenth Step, would turn up the television set while one of the other nameless old men would unplug the jukebox.

I don't mean to imply that Richie Repetition was some sort of folk hero, a drug-addicted Robin Hood, assaulting and selling narcotics to rich and poor alike. No, it was only in the Thirteenth Step that anyone, save the police and his customers, paid him any attention. It was a tribute to their lifelong patronship with Richie Repetition's grandfather, Richard Repetition, who had recently moved on to the perpetual night of the Shirley Goodness Retirement Paradise, where the city's ghosts live. The old men of the Thirteenth Step had watched Richie Repetition grow up, in the bar and on television.

It wasn't far from last call when Richie Repetition and Harold Esquire, Esq. made their television appearances, and Savior Neck had passed out with his head on the hard-wood bar hours before. Anyone else would have been awakened and sent home, but Savior Neck was already, in effect, home—he rented a room on the floor above the Thirteenth Step from Vinnie Domino.

Savior Neck's wrinkled gray face and thin white hair spread themselves out on the dark-stained counter beside his near-empty glass, and he looked, except for the puddle of drool that had slipped from his mouth, like a dead man. At that moment, Savior Neck was a dead man. He'd been a dead man for years.

Harold Esquire, Esq. was by no means capable of resurrecting Savior Neck. He was a lawyer, and resurrection wasn't part of his job description. Had he been something other than a lawyer—a doctor, perhaps, or a faith healer—he still wouldn't have been interested in resurrecting Savior Neck. Even now I can't honestly say what Harold Esquire, Esq. was interested in, aside, perhaps, from publicity, or Penny Dreadful, but frankly, it's none of our concern. We need only know that he didn't resurrect Savior Neck, that he didn't set the story in motion when Vinnie Domino turned up the volume.

Savior Neck did, however, awaken with a shriek and fall off his stool when Vinnie Domino turned up the volume.

"Sshh!" one of the old men mumbled, "Richie's on."

Savior Neck was trembling as he stood up, lifted his glass to his lips, and swallowed it—mostly melted ice, maybe a drop or two of the usual. He put the glass back on the bar, said, "See you tomorrow," to no one in particular, and turned to leave.

"Sshh!" said one of the other old men.

"Where you headed?" said Vinnie Domino.

Savior Neck had decided to take the long way home, since home was upstairs. Perhaps he was drawn outside for some fresh air, or by a desire to stop being dead, or simply to enjoy the beautiful evening. In any case, he wasn't drawn out by delusion, confusion, or amusement. And certainly not by Harold Esquire, Esq.

He bumped into several drunken old men as he walked toward the door. Then he stepped out into the cold Discordant night.

Savior Neck wasn't walking in his sleep. He'd never been one to get very creative with his dreams, always walking and arriving and walking back. The unconscious of the dead is no more imaginative than the conscious.

You remember that Savior Neck was dead. Maybe the discomfort of being lost in a place in which one can't be lost is the discomfort of someone about to be raised from the dead, a Lazarus about to come forth, about to be blessed, or cursed, with new life.

But Lord, he stinketh. Lord does he stinketh.

We should put aside this question of whether resurrection is a blessing or a curse for now. Forever. We can agree without another sniff on the fact that Savior Neck stinketh. When a man has been dead for so much of his life, the threat of resurrection makes him aware of his stink, and he looks about, to see whether anyone else has witnessed the man-made miracle, half expecting the voice of God to boom down from heaven declaring him His beloved son, with whom He is well pleased.

It wasn't God's voice. It was Officer Longarm's. He and his partner had been idling in their patrol car beside Savior Neck for several minutes as Savior Neck stood idling on the road.

Officer Longarm didn't say anything particularly startling, but Savior Neck was startled nonetheless when he said what he said. He was getting anxious in those last few minutes before the first few minutes of the rest of his life.

"What brings you out here this time of night?" said Officer Longarm.

Savior Neck jumped perceptibly, a full-body hiccup. He looked over and recognized Officer Longarm. While Savior Neck wasn't a criminal per se, he had spent a night or two in jail here and there. But he wouldn't have had to do so to recognize Officer Longarm.

For the people of Discord, Officer Longarm was a flesh-and-bone symbol of the law. He'd given them their first speeding tickets, and their children their first speeding tickets, and their children's children and so on, confiscating skateboards from eight-year-old boys when he caught them skateboarding in the public park on a midsummer night, and issuing summonses to those—regardless of age—with open containers in same. He knew them all, and punished them according to their offenses and forgave them once they'd paid their debt to society, and been rehabilitated. Discord is, after all, not such a large city.

Strange then that Savior Neck didn't recognize Officer Longarm's partner, sitting shadowy behind the wheel.

"Just enjoying the beautiful evening," said Savior Neck.

Officer Longarm could tell that Savior Neck was intoxicated.

Savior Neck wasn't intoxicated. He'd only had a drink or two that night.

"It's kinda cold out, isn't it," said Officer Longarm, "to be enjoying this beautiful evening without a coat?"

"Am I breaking any laws?" said Savior Neck.

Officer Longarm tipped his head back as though to consolidate the volumes of legal data that were floating about his brain into one place in the bulb of his skull, then tipped his head back to its original position, rolling the information out of his mouth like ticker tape.

"I'll say no," said Officer Longarm, "even though public intoxication and suicide are both crimes."

Officer Longarm couldn't have known that suicide wasn't really a possibility. As for public intoxication, Savior Neck wasn't publicly intoxicated, unless public intoxication means something other than being intoxicated in public, because he wasn't intoxicated.

"But I'm not drunk," said Savior Neck.

"Sure," said Officer Longarm's partner, his voice barely carrying across Officer Longarm and out into the blizzard.

"Really," said Savior Neck, "I only had a drink or two."

"Why don't you get in the car and let us take you home," said Officer Longarm.

Savior Neck kicked at snow with one foot.

"I'll walk," said Savior Neck, and he walked, away from Discord, leaving a trail of footprints that led out of the valley of the shadow of death, and the officers followed, leaving tire marks that carried no symbolic value.

Officer Longarm's partner pulled the car up beside Savior Neck.

"You're going the wrong way," said Officer Longarm.

"I know where I'm headed," said Savior Neck, who was headed nowhere.

"Then where you going?" said Officer Longarm.

"Home," said Savior Neck.

He continued walking nowhere.

Officer Longarm didn't know where Savior Neck lived, but he knew that Savior Neck lived in Discord; he knew Savior Neck lived downtown, and if you'd put a gun to his head, he probably would have remembered that Savior Neck lived on Main Street above a bar. But there are enough bars on Main Street that he couldn't have guessed that Savior Neck's room was above the Thirteenth Step. Officer Longarm can't be faulted for his fading memory. He wasn't, after all, a computer, and his head was already crammed with those volumes of legal data.

"I thought you lived downtown," said Officer Longarm.

Savior Neck continued walking. He wasn't ignoring Officer Longarm's question as statement. He hadn't heard it. But Officer Longarm's partner hated to be ignored. He revved the engine, sped past Savior Neck, and skidded to a stop, blocking the road with the car.

Savior Neck approached the passenger-side window of the patrol car with an air of curiosity, as though it hadn't skidded to a stop in plain view only moments before, as though he and Officer Longarm hadn't had the rudiments of a conversation only moments before that. Savior Neck stuck his head in.

"Something the matter?" he said

Officer Longarm looked away from Savior Neck, through his partner, out the driver-side window, which was closed.

"Get in the car," said his partner.

He drove back toward Discord at a speed that might have been considered excessive even on a summer evening with a distance of months between the car and the nearest blizzard. The road that led back to town was winding and twisted and coiled, and he had a tendency to accelerate into the curves, despite the snow. Officer Longarm commented on it as they went.

"You've got to speed into these turns," he said, glancing back at Savior Neck, who, to his partner's agitation, was treating them as he might have treated a taxi-driver—someone paid only for the service of driving a person from point A to point B rather than to protect and to serve—and then returning his eyes to the road lest he endanger the three of them by not watching as his partner accelerated into the next turn. "That's why we have to pull so many people over here," he told the windshield. "I don't mind the speeding so much, it's just they don't know to accelerate into the turns."

Savior Neck didn't drive, nor did he spend much time contemplating friction and centrifugal force. He mostly slid back and forth between this turn and that, lost in his own discomfort.

At one particularly jarring turn, his water broke. The piss trickled out of him, and his thighs began to thaw. The pain of cocoa after building a snowman, of a chilled glass filled with hot water, where extremes meet at the ends of a line disguised as a circle, and freezers burn spread across his loins, and he prepared to deliver himself, not into the gentle hands of a physician, but into the Longarm of the law.

"Do you have any napkins?" said Savior Neck.

Officer Longarm made no reply as his partner accelerated into the turn that became Main Street.

Lord He Still Stinketh

Savior Neck looked up at the window of his room. The car had been idling for some time, and Officer Longarm was turning his head, looking now at this bar, now at that, wondering which one Savior Neck called home. He had just about given up hope of Savior Neck's telling him, but he continued to ask, "Which one's yours?"

The car was warm, too warm for discomfort. The fan blew hot air through the interior. The smell of urine floated along the currents, ricocheted against the back window, split, and circled the heads of the officers, stopping beneath their nostrils. Officer Longarm and his partner sniffed. They made wasn't-me shows of sniffing.

Officer Longarm's partner glanced back toward Savior Neck, but saw very little in the blue glare cast by the streetlamps, nothing to confirm that the smell that had stopped beneath his nostrils was indeed the smell of urine. He moved for the light switch, and thought better of it. He reached across Officer Longarm to the glove box, pulled out a small pile of napkins, and lobbed them over his shoulder.

"A drink or two," he said.

He put the car in drive, and headed down Main Street. City Hall awaited him and his partner and baby Savior Neck at the end.

Katz Talks

"Some holiday cheer?" he offered.

It wasn't Officer Longarm, but he was an officer. Not much of an officer. Not an officer who took his duties very seriously, by the looks of him—face flushed, hair unkempt, shirt untucked, left shoe untied, holster unsnapped. Officer Longarm never looked holiday cheerful, especially not while on duty, but, again, it wasn't Officer Longarm. It was his partner. And it wasn't the holidays.

He had his arm between the bars. The hand at the end of the arm held the mug of holiday cheer. Savior Neck made no move to take it.

"Really," said the officer, "drink up. Merry Christmas."

Savior Neck was standing in the middle of the cell. At his feet lay the change of secondhand clothes that Officer Longarm had taken from the locker they used as a lost and found, and offered him.

"Okay." The officer bent down unsteadily and placed the mug of holiday cheer beside the change of clothes. "I'll just leave it right here. Case you want it."

The officer walked back across the room to where several other officers were clustered around a desk, each with his own mug.

"I wouldn't drink that if I were you," said Joey Katz.

Savior Neck turned around.

"Joey Katz," said Joey Katz, offering his hand, without looking him in the eyes. His own eyes were on the officer's own waist.

Savior Neck accepted, but didn't offer "Savior Neck" in return.

He didn't know Joey Katz. Strange. Everyone in Discord knows everyone else in Discord, especially folks who travel in the same circles. Savior Neck, being the type who spent the occasional night in a police-station holding cell, ought then, to have known Joey Katz, who was spending that occasional night in a police-station holding cell.

"You're not from around here, are you," said Joey Katz.

"I was gonna say the same of you," said Savior Neck.

"Me?" said Joey Katz, surprised to the point of taking offense. "I live just up the road. A room above a bar."

"Same here," said Savior Neck, forgetting, for a moment, his resurrection discomfort.

"You're shitting me," said Joey Katz, again with that accusatory expression of surprise.

"No," said Savior Neck, "Really. The Thirteenth..."

"Never heard of it," said Joey Katz.

Joey Katz backed himself casually into the corner with his hands in his pockets, and rested a shoulder blade against each wall. The surprise had left his face, leaving his intricate features to fend unsuccessfully for themselves.

"I was just saying," said Joey Katz, though his lips didn't seem to be moving, and if they were, nothing else was, "I wouldn't drink that if I were you."

Savior Neck scanned the room, looking for what Joey Katz wouldn't drink if he were him. He'd already forgotten about the holiday cheer, still puzzled as to how Joey Katz could have lived up the road, Main Street, he presumed, in a room above a bar, and never heard of the Thirteenth Step. His eyes stopped at the mug. Eggnog, mixed with god-knows-what. That long after Christmas it couldn't have been any good.

"That?" said Savior Neck, "I wouldn't drink it if I were me, either."

He bent down, picked up the secondhand clothes that

lay beside the mug, and unfolded them. There was a wrinkled t-shirt with a frayed right sleeve, and a pair of slacks that were—it was already clear—several sizes too large. He began to change, turning his back to Joey Katz out of modesty.

"Still, I'm just saying," said Joey Katz, "it's a good thing you don't want it, 'cause if you did, I'd have to strongly recommend you not drink it."

"Well, I don't," said Savior Neck. "I won't. So it's settled."

"Yep," said Joey Katz, "all settled, just so long as you don't want it later, either. Drinking it later's just as bad as drinking it now. Maybe worse."

Savior Neck adjusted his new outfit, pulling the belt from the discarded pants and tightening it in order to keep the lost-and-found slacks from ending up around his ankles. He picked up the mug.

"Are you trying to tell me you want it?" said Savior Neck.

"O contrare, moan frair," said Joey Katz with an exaggerated shake of the head, "I wouldn't drink that for a million bucks. It's poison."

"You don't have to tell me twice," said Savior Neck.

The direction the conversation had taken was pushing Savior Neck back toward his habitual role of old dead drunk, and he lifted the mug of holiday cheer to his lips reflexively. Joey Katz was happy to have another chance to disapprove.

"I'm telling you," said Joey Katz, "I wouldn't drink that if I were you."

"Well it turns out," said Savior Neck, "you're not me," and he took an unhealthy gulp of holiday cheer.

"Now you've done it!" said Joey Katz. "You've really gone and done it, now. Swallowing poison like it was rotten eggnog!"

Savior Neck was caught off guard. He hadn't swallowed poison like it was rotten eggnog. He'd swallowed rotten eggnog like it was poison.

"You didn't believe me?" said Joey Katz. "You didn't believe it was poisoned? Was it even worth it to take the chance?"

"What're you talking about?" said Savior Neck.

Joey Katz calmed down, suddenly as subdued as he had been livid a moment before.

"You just carried out your own death sentence," he said.

"I'm not following you," said Savior Neck.

"Why do you think you're in here?" he said.

Savior Neck drew a blank to match the one that led him to the police station.

"You're condemned to death!" said Joey Katz.

"Bullshit." Savior Neck laughed uncomfortably, not because he believed, or even understood, what Joey Katz was telling him, but because he was nervous about spending the night in a holding cell with such a crackpot.

"I knew you didn't believe me," said Joey Katz. "They knew you wouldn't believe me, too. Just ask the cops. Ask the cops why you're here. Hey," he yelled across the room at the officers, who were still nursing their holiday cheer, "Why's this guy here?"

Officer Longarm's partner looked over his shoulder.

"What?" he said.

"Why. Is. This. Guy. In. Here?" said Joey Katz.

"His mommy wanted us to potty-train him," said Officer Longarm's partner, and the other officers burst into laughter.

"You're condemned to death," said Joey Katz. "They don't put people in jail to be potty-trained."

Savior Neck couldn't have explained why he'd begun to feel dizzy without giving credence to Joey Katz's ramblings.

He wasn't drunk. He'd had a drink or two, hours before, and the holiday cheer, of which he'd taken only a gulp, was pretty light on the cheer. He stumbled backward and caught himself.

"They were talking about it before you got here," said Joey Katz.

Savior Neck's vision blurred. He tried to pick the real Joey Katz from among the three that surrounded him.

"At first I thought it was me," said Joey Katz. "Talking about some guy rents a room above a bar, pick him up, condemn him to death. Almost wet my pants, too."

Savior Neck leaned against the wall. His stomach turned and he doubled over. There was a pain in his chest and a gasping for breath. He vomited violently, from his mouth, his nose, his eyes.

"That's the best thing to do," said Joey Katz. "Induce vomiting, get it all out of your system."

Savior Neck fell to the floor on hands and knees.

"Then I realized they weren't using my name," said Joey Katz, resuming his monologue. "Vinnie Something-or-other. He was in on it, part of the setup. And then the other guy, the guy who's condemned to death. Savior Neck. That's you, right?"

Savior Neck couldn't confirm his deductions. He was already out cold.

The Ghosts of Goodness

Savior Neck awoke beneath an old afghan. It was long enough to cover his feet, but they were cold, having slipped through a large hole and out into the room. His eyes were blurry with sleep, but he could still make out the browns, oranges, and yellows of the blanket, like something somebody's granny would crochet. Like something his granny would have crocheted.

Savior Neck awoke, beneath an afghan that his granny had crocheted long before her long-ago death, on a sofa in his father's room in the Shirley Goodness Retirement Paradise, which was not actually a paradise, but a large concrete structure that appeared to have been built by fascists, like almost every building constructed in Discord, New York, since the second world war, though I don't wish to imply that Discord experienced a postwar architectural boom.

He pulled off the afghan and let it fall to the floor, then sat up. He was wearing his own clothes, the same ones, in fact, that he had worn on what he could only assume was the previous night. They were, however, freshly laundered, and radiated the industrial smell of spring rather than the usual aura of stale cigarette smoke that Savior Neck wore like perfume.

He reached up to the breast pocket of his shirt, and pulled out his cigarettes. He looked around for an ashtray, but found none. Savior Neck lit one and inhaled deeply, still looking about the room—which was finally coming into focus, or what passed for focus in Savior Neck's eyes—for some receptacle.

He walked through the room, slowing once to drop a long ash in the trash can, and stopped at the window, one pane of which was broken and patched with cardboard. The sun shown blindingly on the snow below, and glistened on the already slushy streets. Road salt and city traffic make short work of even the worst blizzards in Discord. He peeled up the square of cardboard, and threw out the butt. He lost sight of it before it ever hit the gritty gray powder.

Cold, bright air streamed in through the window. Musty, stagnant air hovered in the room. They met before Savior Neck and melted the sky. He couldn't remember how he'd gotten there.

Savior Neck walked back to the tattered sofa, and sat down. He assumed his father was asleep behind the sheet that divided the room, but didn't want to wake him. He didn't want to see his father.

He remembered passing out in a jail cell in another man's clothes, but beyond that—nothing. Whether or not it was the next day, he couldn't be sure. For all he knew or could say, he'd Rip Van Winkled himself out of his own poisoning death, as though some cold, cold nitrogen in the eggnog had frozen his resurrection in time while he was wheelchaired through space and changes of clothing to awaken years later beneath an afghan on a sofa in a room in the Shirley Goodness Retirement Paradise.

And then there was the possibility that he'd been poisoned to death. He was in the Shirley Goodness Retirement Paradise after all.

It was the next day. He was as alive as his rebirth could get him.

He pulled the afghan over his legs. The room was growing cold. He could see his breath in front of his face. A cat, his father's, leapt into Savior Neck's lap to warm itself. Savior Neck looked down at it. It looked up at Savior Neck, smugly, as though it had more right than he to be there, as though it was warming Savior Neck rather than vice versa. It yawned, its breath visibly rolling out of its mouth toward Savior Neck's nostrils. He almost gagged when he smelled it. He grabbed the cat's face, forcing its mouth closed with two fingers, looking into its eyes.

There was a knock at the apartment door, the cat jumped off of him, and the door opened. Savior Neck recognized the woman standing in the doorway: his father's nurse. She was greeted by a blast of cold air from the broken window.

Her shriek added to Savior Neck's conviction that he had no right or reason to be there, that someone had simply plucked him from one scene and placed him in another. He tensed as though to hide a nakedness covered only by his clothes. Any conscious person could have seen through him, past him, exaggerated or altogether ignored his shame. The nurse didn't see through him.

"Oh," she said, putting her hand to her heart. "I forgot you were here."

She breathed heavily, dramatically, to show him that his presence had been, but shouldn't have been, a surprise, and crossed the threshold to the window on the other side of the room.

"Your father usually likes it a bit warmer in here," she said, replacing the cardboard, trying not to sound accusatory. "A little too warm if you ask me," commiserating with Savior Neck, at least to her way of seeing things, "but that's how he likes it."

Savior Neck was having a hard time digesting the fact that she'd only been momentarily surprised, that she wasn't treating him as an intruder. Still, he glanced around the room to give the cat an I-told-you-so glare. The cat had disappeared.

The nurse walked back across the room and shut the

door. Then she walked over to the metal trash can in the rear corner of the room, and said, "I'm gonna make your father his lunch. Want something?"

"Does he know I'm here?" said Savior Neck.

"Does who know you're here?" she said.

"My father," said Savior Neck.

She stared at him as though it were an odd question.

"He was still asleep when you came in," she said. "It doesn't sound like he's up yet."

She resumed whatever it was she was doing, intending, apparently, for lack of any other instruction, to cook for both his father and Savior Neck.

"How'd I get here?" said Savior Neck.

"Don't look at me," she said.

Savior Neck took her reply literally. He turned back to the window, and watched the occasional car slush the slush.

"Sorry," he said.

"Oh, I don't mind," she said, misunderstanding. "I take care of so many old folks around here, its kind of nice to see someone my own age for once," as though she and Savior Neck were not old folks.

She seemed to consider that the end of the conversation. She took some paper from the floor, crumpled it, dropped it into the trash can, and followed it with a lit match. Fire began to crackle within, echoing off the metal walls, and soon, smoke was billowing out into the room.

Savior Neck lit another cigarette, walked over to the window, and removed the cardboard, still wondering how he'd gotten there, not the window, but his father's room, on the top floor of the Shirley Goodness Retirement Paradise. He was certain his father's nurse was just being delicate, that she assumed he'd been on another binge, which had somehow ended on his father's couch. It wouldn't have been the first time.

He wanted to speak up, to tell her he hadn't been drinking, but he'd used that line before, on several of the previous occasions when he'd awakened there at the end of a binge. Besides, the last thing he could remember was drinking rotten eggnog as though it were poison, so he couldn't honestly say he hadn't been drinking.

"I'm condemned to death," said Savior Neck.

She didn't hear him. She was busy with her makeshift grill. Savior Neck heard the cat wail from behind the curtain, as though in pain or anger. Then he heard his father wail as though in pain or anger, and rather than wait for his father to storm out, find the no-good son who'd put him in this godforsaken shithole, and begin ranting about the kind of son who would put him in this godforsaken shithole, Savior Neck escaped from this godforsaken shithole.

Baby Steps Toward a New Usual

Outside in the cold again, without a coat, Savior Neck walked a bit more loosely, almost like a real person, though perhaps a little wobbly. Gone was the discomfort of the night before. He was trying out his new legs.

He passed people on the street. Sometimes he knew them and sometimes he didn't. He recognized them all, but they were all different, maybe a shade brighter or a shade darker. It doesn't much matter, because the difference was marginal and he was barely conscious of it anyway.

Outside the Thirteenth Step, he gazed through the window, saw Vinnie Domino, and shivered. There's nothing strange about shivering. It was cold out and Savior Neck wasn't wearing a coat. Vinnie Domino was talking to a woman at the bar. Nothing terribly strange about that, either. Sometimes people that Savior Neck didn't know stopped into the Thirteenth Step for a drink. Never a woman, as far as he could remember, but still this was no more unusual than the usual unusual. He shivered again. He went around to the alley and climbed up the fire escape, and what's so strange about that? Savior Neck used the fire escape all the time in the summer. It wasn't quite spring. The railings were slick with melting ice. Savior Neck shivered.

That night, Savior Neck did his drinking in his room, running down the fire escape, to the store and quickly back, three separate times, though it might have been more had the gas-station clerk not performed his civic duty by enforcing laws as blue as Savior Neck's skin beneath the streetlamps on the unfated night before. He felt no drive to revive his social life. Or death. Any semantic confusion proves my point: observing the monotonous rotation of the earth on its axis from within a closed system, Savior Neck tried to feel his new self to be much the same as his old, to forget his conviction and subsequent life.

Cat Talks

So it was, on that much-the-same night, also unfated, somewhere between winter and spring, when it's more likely to rain than to snow, and yet the air's bite is still much more fierce than the roar of March's lion, and the lambs are hibernating, or doing whatever it is lambs do in the cold, that Savior Neck fell asleep in a shiny wreath of beer cans and junk-food wrappers. He'd left the window open on returning from the store, and the weather had leaked itself in, filling the room with freeze. Steam rose from Savior Neck's nostrils and hovered above his head, spelling out words and phrases and taking the forms of the lethargic monsters in his dreams.

But no one was there to notice this phenomenon, except for his father's cat, slinking about the perimeters of the room as though it had more right to be there than he did, which wasn't the case. It would stop, now and again, and yawn leisurely, and the same thing would happen: words and phrases spelled out in the steam from its rotting guts.

Savior Neck awoke from uneventful dreams, in which, as usual, he walked to the Discordant Falls and back, to find his room filled with the shit-stinking mist of the cat's breath, and the walls papered with a vapor-message:

"Don't tell anyone else," said the breath on the walls.

The cat leaped onto Savior Neck's bed and stared him down. Savior Neck was quick to look away, covering his nose and his mouth lest he gag. That cat had hell in its belly.

"Don't tell anyone else what?" said Savior Neck.

Savior Neck looked back to find the cat standing on its hind legs.

"Don't tell anyone else," the cat was speaking now, "that you're condemned to death, or else..."

Or else what? Savior Neck would never know, because the cat delivered a powerful left that sent Savior Neck back to the land of Nod, where he resumed walking, back and forth to his heart's discontent.

A New Usual

As Savior Neck awoke the next morning from the same dream he found himself transformed in his bed into a human being of average size. But that's where the average ends. Most humans don't wake up with an aching in the head that radiates from the right eye. Nor do they generally wake up with memories of having been knocked out by a cat.

The cat! Savior Neck leaped from his bed and stood on the litter-ridden floor, glancing about for signs of the filthy thing. No shit, no hairballs, no pawprints, no trace. No more words devil-breathed on the walls. That terrible stench the only sign at all that it had ever been in his apartment.

Savior Neck got on his hands and knees among the empties and chocolate-smeared Ho Ho packaging and peered beneath the bed, expecting to see two smoky, gleaming eyes, but found only a stack of those papers that someone left outside his room every morning. He never opened them, never even looked at them. Part of the problem.

He stood up, shivered, and closed the window. There would be no more cats, or any other sort of animals, save, perhaps, cockroaches, spiders, and the occasional rat in his apartment, and even then there would have to be some sort of screening process to insure that they were not the types of cockroaches, spiders, and occasional rats who would deliver powerful lefts to humans of average size after reminding them of nearly forgotten condemnations to death. But reminded he was, and no screening process could reverse that. No, that would take a soaking process.

Savior Neck put on a pair of jeans—a shirt slipped his

mind—and went downstairs to do some catching up with Vinnie Something-or-other, who would have to be in on it, who would have to help him drown his knowledge.

Soaking Process

"Long time no see," said Vinnie Domino, who, though it was well shy of noon and the doors were still locked, stood behind the bar as though waiting for someone to order a drink.

Savior Neck bellied up, and gave him a reason to live: the usual. A glass of the usual. The television was on, one of those morning talk shows that are always tiptoeing the line between yawns and chaos. Savior Neck swallowed his drink in a cartoon gulp and lit a cigarette.

"What have you been up to?" said Vinnie Domino.

It wasn't small talk. Vinnie Domino italicized the what up for me.

"The usual," said Savior Neck.

"I never seen nothing like that on your face," said Vinnie Domino, stepping out of Savior Neck's way so he could see himself in the mirror behind the bar, the shiner on the unfamiliar face staring him in the black eye.

Savior Neck watched the left hand in the mirror move toward the face; he watched the face wince as he winced.

"I guess I got punched," said Savior Neck, as though he'd really needed to see the bruise to know.

On cue, the talk show erupted suddenly into violence, and just as suddenly spilled into the realm of telephone psychicology, where a large, a positively fat old woman comforted Snow White with visions of Prince Financial Security.

"He got punched in the face," said Vinnie Domino to a Thirteenth Step full of men who, for him, were always there, whether or not they were there.

"He got punched in the face," they might have echoed.

"Of course you got punched in the face!" said Vinnie Domino. "But who punched you? Where? When? Why! This guy misses a night at my bar for the first time in I don't know how long even though he lives right upstairs. I'm thinking maybe he's cleaning himself up; taking a step back, laying off the poison. Then he comes back half-naked with a black eye, and he ain't even gonna tell me what happened! Gives me a good mind to kick a man outta here on his skinny ass," he said. To his audience of none.

"Another one," said Savior Neck, clocking the bottom of his empty glass on the counter.

Madame Mammy finished solving the world's relationship problems, and passed the torch to Harold Esquire, Esq.

"This one's on the house," said Vinnie Domino, "if you let an old man in on it."

When really they were all on the house. The only foreseeable problem with Savior Neck's born-again lifestyle was the high cost of cheap beer at the convenience store where, no matter how much bitching and muttering, muttering and bitching he did, they wouldn't allow him a tab. Savior Neck's tab at the Thirteenth Step ran to several hundred wide-ruled pages of one two three four slash-fives. At the Thirteenth Step, before the fire at least, Savior Neck had dangled a small inheritance in potentia before Vinnie Domino's eyes that was enough to keep him penciling primitive marks on yellowing pages, and it had ended in its continuance, becoming a habit, an empty ritual.

"It's a long story," said Savior Neck. "It all started a couple nights ago..."

"Hang on," said Vinnie Domino. "Richie."

There had been a sharp increase in those times at the Thirteenth Step when the weak mumble became the expectant silence as their no-longer-little protégé appeared on screen, his fifteen minutes spread out in repeating thirty-second segments, since Harold Esquire, Esq. had begun airing commercials between the hootin' and hollerin' of the *Hootin' and Hollerin' Show* and the wise and comforting advice of your Aunt Remus. And bar policy was bar policy, operating hours or not.

"Harold Esquire, Esq. solved all of my legal problems," said a suspiciously calm and clean-cut Richie Repetition with all of the robotic conviction of a man who truly believes what he's saying placed in front of a camera.

Harold Esquire, Esq., on the other hand, was smooth and confident, a perpetual legal motion machine. He walked onscreen and put his hand on Richie Repetition's shoulder. Vinnie Domino crossed himself and turned back to Savior Neck.

"What that man did for that boy," said Vinnie Domino, as though all present were well acquainted with what that man did for that boy.

"What?" said Savior Neck. "Get him out of jail?"

"No," said Vinnie Domino, "fixed him for good. Look at him all clean-shaved, nice haircut, wearing a suit. He's a different boy. A straightened-out boy. Got his act together."

"He'll be back in soon enough," said Savior Neck.

Vinnie Domino's eyes flared with an anger they didn't often flare with. He was a pretty congenial guy. A little gruff, but never really angry. Not usually angry. He poked a finger into Savior Neck's bare chest.

"What're you trying to say?" said Vinnie Domino.

Savior Neck leaned back so Vinnie Domino's finger was merely poking at his chest, as opposed to puncturing, and raised his hands in a gesture of peace or surrender.

"Sorry," said Savior Neck. "Does this mean no free drink?"

Vinnie Domino poured the usual into a clean glass and

placed it in front of Savior Neck. Savior Neck raised the glass to his lips. Another psychic on television was predicting the future with baseball cards. The bodybuilders and washed-up golf pros he advised were crying like babies.

"What?" said Savior Neck.

"Dish," said Vinnie Domino taking the glass from Savior Neck's hand and holding firmly against the bar.

Savior Neck considered how best to tell his old friend, his landlord, his bartender, Vinnie Domino, that he'd been beaten up by his father's cat.

"It's a long story," said Savior Neck, "so I'll start from scratch. The police..."

Ah, how convenient. How fortunate. How unembarrassing for him.

"The police?" said Vinnie Domino.

In his surprise, Vinnie Domino let go of the glass, and Savior Neck snatched it and swallowed the drink as quickly as he would have had he still been a dead man.

"Yeah," said Savior Neck, "the police. The other night. That big..."

"The police did that to you?" said Vinnie Domino.

The police didn't do that to you. Not directly. Officer Longarm didn't. Punch you in the eye. The cat did. But the cat told you. Don't tell anyone. That you're condemned to death. Or else... So the cat was in on it too. An agent of the police. Officer Longarm's right paw. Yeah, the police did that to you.

"Yeah," said Savior Neck, "the police did it."

The psychic predicted another lawyer commercial and voila—the virtual entrality of Harold Esquire, Esq., Discord's foremost general legal practitioner and demi-celebrity.

Richie Repetition

(*suspiciously calm*) Harold Esquire Esquire solved all of my legal troubles.

Vinnie Domino

...and he can solve yours too.

Cut to: *Hootin' and Hollerin' Show* and...

Fade to gray. (soon enough)

Noon

Savior Neck walked stumble-drunk down the stairs, spinning and swaying to the rhythm of a lush Discord morning. The drinking I've recorded was just the beginning. It was followed by: a free drink for the ordeal of police brutality (A man who's been through what you been through deserves a drink just for living to tell the tale) (Of course, we know he was alive but hadn't yet told a tale, much less the tail), a free drink for admitting that Harold Esquire, Esq. might be able to do something about his situation (He is a lawyer after all), a free drink for promising to march on down to Harold Esquire, Esq.'s (conveniently located) basement office as soon as he'd taken care of this business of drowning his knowledge (What do you got better to do), and two free drinks for the one: courage and two: stamina to do that marching (and walk on in with your head held high).

He bumped against the railing and slipped on steps, watching the stuttering shuffle of his shoes across slabs of cement. Sometimes he lost his precarious balance, swung full circle, and landed on a crack. His breath steamed in the cold, but it was an illiterate steam and he was feeling too warm to shiver.

Harold Esquire, Esq.'s office was located directly below the Thirteenth Step. Savior Neck stared cross-eyed at his reflection in the door. He backed up headfirst. The window's version of his bare chest read:

Harold Esquire, Esq.
General Legal Practitioner

The lights were out. He tried the handle. The door was locked. A little sign on his reflection's stomach read:

Will return at

Savior Neck looked down the block at the big clock outside the bank. It read:

He was beginning to get cold. A half shiver. He leaned against the reflection of his naked back, and slept the whole squeaky way down.

After Noon

Savior Neck awoke to a kick in the ribs, and jumped to his feet. He recognized Officer Longarm. Backed into a corner. Behind Officer Longarm, Harold Esquire, Esq. Savior Neck realized they were in cahoots. So the lawyers were in on it. He wondered whether there might be anyone in Discord who wasn't in cahoots. The only thing worse than being condemned to death is being the only one not in cahoots.

"You all right?" said Officer Longarm.

Savior Neck bolted past Officer Longarm, tripped over Harold Esquire, Esq.'s briefcase, and went sprawling into the middle of Main Street. The briefcase toppled over and spilled its contents: an empty hip-flask, a supermarket tabloid, a roll of clear tape, and a deck of playing cards. A car screeched to a stop inches from Savior Neck's right foot, and he was quickly lifted and dragged into Harold Esquire, Esq.'s office.

Wrong Number

Harold Esquire, Esq. paced back and forth in front of Savior Neck with his briefcase held open before him like a hymnal. Pre-interrogation hymn number one two three: "For Christ's Sake Keep Thine Fucking Mouth Shut."

"You didn't see this," said Harold Esquire, Esq., was saying, "YOU didn't see this you DIDN'T see this you didn't SEE this you didn't see THIS SO FOR CHRIST'S SAKE KEEP THINE FUCKING MOUTH SHUT," in the key of very loud.

Savior Neck sat in a molded plastic chair, his hands dangling at his sides, his eyes following Harold Esquire, Esq. with all of the comprehension of a medieval peasant at high mass.

"I didn't see what?" said Savior Neck.

Harold Esquire, Esq. dropped his hymnal on the floor and stomped toward Savior Neck. Then he stomped away from Savior Neck, picked up his briefcase, closed it, and stomped back toward Savior Neck.

"What is this?" said Harold Esquire, Esq., shoving the briefcase beneath Savior Neck's nose so that Savior Neck couldn't tell whether the smell of liquor was a reflection of his own breath or something ingrained in the faux-leather.

"Briefcase," said Savior Neck.

"And this?" said Harold Esquire, Esq. pressing the buttons that opened the briefcase so the top hit Savior Neck's forehead and the bridge of his nose, and he knew that though Harold Esquire, Esq. didn't live above a bar on Main Street, and wasn't a patron of the Thirteenth Step, someone had managed to polish his briefcase with some very potent liquor.

Harold Esquire, Esq. jerked the briefcase from Savior Neck's face, and held it about a foot in front of him, pointing at something inside.

"Newspaper," said Savior Neck.

At something else.

"Pocket-rocket," said Savior Neck, "empty."

As well as, "A roll of scotch tape and," in anticipation of Harold Esquire, Esq.'s next move, "a deck of playing cards."

"None of which you saw," said Harold Esquire, Esq., closing the briefcase one last time, and throwing it across the room, where it hit the wall, popped open, and spilled its contents. One last time.

"None of which I saw?" said Savior Neck, glancing across the room at nothing he could see. "I guess I'll just keep mine fucking mouth shut about nothing I didn't see."

"If you're smart," said Harold Esquire, Esq.

He straightened his hair and adjusted his suit, then he bowed his head and placed the bridge of his nose between his thumb and index finger.

"I'm sorry," he said, reaching into his back pocket. "I've just been under a lot of stress lately."

He pulled a one-dollar bill from his wallet, lifted one of Savior Neck's dangling arms, and placed the cash in his hand.

"Go get yourself something to eat," said Harold Esquire, Esq.

"But..." said Savior Neck.

"What? Not good enough?" said Harold Esquire, Esq., half agitated.

He gave him another one-dollar bill. Savior Neck sat looking up at him.

"Here then," said Harold Esquire, Esq., and handed him a five-dollar bill.

He opened the lips of the wallet and turned it upside

down to show that it was empty.

"I'm not hungry," said Savior Neck.

Harold Esquire, Esq. shoved the wallet back in his pocket and glared at Savior Neck.

"Then spend it on alcohol!" he said. "I don't give a damn what you do with it! Just get the hell out of here and don't camp out in front of my office anymore!"

"The sign," said Savior Neck. "It said you'd be back at noon."

Harold Esquire, Esq. stomped over to the telephone.

"Listen." Near-silence, a faint dial-tone floating along the room's imperceptible air currents. "I'm calling the cops."

Savior Neck was up, stiff, a human caught in the cahooting headlights of a late-night legal system. He inched toward the door and extended his hand plaintively, as though begging Harold Esquire, Esq. not to batter him with the receiver. Harold Esquire, Esq. dialed a number quickly, familiarly.

"I'll tell them," said Savior Neck.

"Tell who what?" said Harold Esquire, Esq.

"Discord Police Department" drifted across those imperceptible air currents, and for a moment after, there was silence. "Discord Police Department," said the telephone, "hello?"

Harold Esquire, Esq. made like he was going to respond.

"What I saw," said Savior Neck, "about your briefcase."

"You must have the wrong number, sir," said the earpiece.

Click, dial-tone.

Harold Esquire, Esq. was already across the room, already had Savior Neck by his bare shoulders, shaking and shoving the shirtless vagrant who'd seen too much. A knee to the gut. Another to the jaw. Doubled over in pain. An uppercut straight to the left eye. Mister tattletale was out for the count.

Je Ne Sais Quoi

Savior Neck awoke in a puddle dripped from a dropper, one drop at a time, right between his swollen eyes, trickling down the sides of his face to stagnate like thin, room-temperature blood on the cold tiled mattress we call: floor. Harold Esquire, Esq. stood above him, rhythmically squeezing the red-rubber bulb connected to the tapering tube and chanting, "Wake up, wake up, wake up," in counterpoint.

Savior Neck blinked the water from his eyes, remaining on his back. Harold Esquire, Esq. ceased his mantra, ceased squeezing the bulb, and changed his tune.

"You're alive! You're alive! You're alive, you're up," he said. "I didn't kill you!"

Savior Neck's jaw felt tingly-numb. He spoke with his lips and tongue.

"Weren't you supposed to?" he said.

Harold Esquire, Esq. was caught off guard, and he stopped celebrating so quickly he nearly fell over. But he wasn't upset. He understood that it was his duty as a practitioner of any conceivable, and some inconceivable, generalities and speshyalities of law to instill an understanding of responsible citizenship in those with whom he came in contact, be they clients or be they bums. It was the very least he could do, considering.

"On the contrary," said Harold Esquire, Esq., "my job is to defend anyone who might have killed you, that is killed a person, since you're a person, against the accusation of murder."

"But you're in on it," said Savior Neck through his teeth.

"Again you're mistaken," said Harold Esquire, Esq. "It would be just as illegal for me to be quote-unquote in on it, as you say, as it would for me to simply murder you. In fact, if I were going to bother being in on it, I would just go ahead and murder you since, without someone like myself to defend myself though I suppose I could defend myself..."

"So you are going to kill me," said Savior Neck.

So quick to lose his sense of the sanctity of life. There's nothing worse for the celebration of the absolution of self-imposed murder charges than the would-have-been victim's insistence on being murdered again.

"Just quit it," said Harold Esquire, Esq., "or I'll give you another black... Oh, I guess that would be imp... I didn't punch your right eye. Who else is punching you?"

"That's why I'm here," said Savior Neck

"To get matching black eyes," said Harold Esquire, Esq.

Savior Neck propped himself up on one elbow, and rubbed his jaw. He tried moving it and groaned in pain. Harold Esquire, Esq. squatted swiftly.

"Here, take it easy," he said. "Why don't you lie back down," he said, easing him onto the tiles. "Is there anything I can get for you? A cup of coffee? A shirt?"

He started to unbutton his own shirt, but fumbled, finally ripping it apart, and spreading it across Savior Neck's scrawny chest. It was much too large anyway, Harold Esquire, Esq. having always been on the flabby side.

The situation was more and less serious than he'd thought. Savior Neck, whom he didn't yet know to be Savior Neck, was not murdered. He had, however, sustained some injuries due to (let us amuse ourselves by speaking his language) Harold Esquire, Esq.'s overexcitement. youthful vigor. enthusiasm. je ne sais quoi. On top of this, the man had seen the contents of his briefcase, which, should they have been revealed, could have had damaging effects on his practice. Harold Esquire, Esq. was willing to do anything it took to ensure his uninsurable reputation:

"What can I do for you?" said Harold Esquire, Esq.

Give Up

They had to begin while the wounds were fresh. The public loves it when you bleed all over them, and that's where the case is really tried: the public. Literally. We'll give'em what they want. Heads'll roll before we're through.

To Savior Neck, walking aimlessly again about town, checking his watch every few seconds to be sure that time wasn't escaping it, there almost seemed to be an electricity in the air. He was wearing a clean gray suit, a flower in his lapel, smooth shaven with the occasional nick for good measure, white hair combed back, perhaps a bit thicker? Excitement. Trembling—electricity? Sobriety.

Yes, sobriety. Harold Esquire, Esq. had insisted on his sobriety. Also on the clean suit. He'd even given him the flower. The shave and a haircut were Savior Neck's own two bits. He checked his watch again. Still too much time.

His eyes were nearly swollen shut, as blue-black as pasty-white skin gets. None of those shades of yellow or lilac that imply, in their sickly-looking way, recovery. In order to keep the shiners shiny, Harold Esquire, Esq. had taken a few more shots at him before bidding him good-bye that afternoon, and suggested that Savior Neck might want to lump himself a time or two the next morning. This morning. The present past. Twenty hours later.

Twenty hours without a drop to drink, not a wink, or a throb of sleep, a whole night without closing his eyes, afraid that he might not be able to open them again, to keep a lookout for talking cats. Seven dollars burning a hole in Savior Neck's pocket, seven of Harold Esquire, Esq.'s dollars, and still not a sip. The lengths to which we'll go to avoid our death sentences. Or is it still police brutality?

Savior Neck, what are we going to do with you? How can we ease your suffering if we don't know your suffering? Do you know how hard it is for us to collect all of your dispersals, to disperse all of your collections? Sometimes I feel like giving up. Sometimes I just give up.

Reminder

Savior Neck landed on the ground and jumped back up as quickly as his old body could. He brushed himself off. The gravel left a gray chalk on his palms and blended into the fabric of his suit. He picked up the flower that had fallen from his lapel, but didn't replace it. It was withered and old already, like Savior Neck.

He looked around, to see if anyone had been watching, to see what had caused his fall from graceless. There was a pair of legs stretched out directly behind him, attached to the torso leaning against the wall of the overpass, attached to a face that betrayed no knowledge of having just tripped a man.

Savior Neck thought he recognized the face, that of an old-looking young man, attached to a gasoline can. He walked over and sat beside him, stretching out his own legs when in Rome. They looked like two peas in a pod at the bottom of the produce bin in a supermarket so far from where peas are grown that even the peas on top are long past fresh. Two pairs of outstretched legs. Two less-than-fashionable suits. Two pairs of black eyes. Thomas Didymus didn't notice the similarities. Or Savior Neck's presence.

"What're you doing there?" said Savior Neck.

Thomas Didymus inhaled deeply and coughed until he heaved. Savior Neck patted him on the back.

"What's that?" said Savior Neck.

Thomas Didymus passed the can slowly to Savior Neck. Savior Neck sniffed at the tube that funneled from it. There was gasoline in that gasoline can.

"It's gasoline," said Savior Neck

He put the can beside him, away from Thomas Didymus, and turned his attention to the withered flower in his hand, twirling it between thumb and forefinger. Thomas Didymus tapped his arm and pointed it at nothing Savior Neck could see. Savior Neck offered him the flower, but Thomas Didymus made no move to accept. He tapped Savior Neck's arm again and pointed again at nothing again that Savior Neck could see.

Savior Neck looked about him, still twirling the flower between thumb and forefinger. His eyes stopped on the gas can.

"This?" He picked it up and showed it to Thomas Didymus.

Thomas Didymus didn't respond, but didn't tap Savior Neck's arm again.

Savior Neck sniffed at the tube that funneled from the can. He sniffed at the withered flower. He doused the withered flower with gasoline, and handed the can back to Thomas Didymus. He sniffed the flower he'd doused.

"It seems," said Savior Neck, "like this is the smell of my own death."

He twirled it beneath his nose, inhaling deeply, and coughed until he heaved. Thomas Didymus patted him on the back, too slowly to do any good.

"Thanks," said Savior Neck, sputtering.

Thomas Didymus was gazing absently in the other direction.

"It turns out I'm condemned to death," said Savior Neck. "Death by police brutality."

He sniffed the flower again.

"They tell the cat what to do," he said. "Also my lawyer. They're all in on it. Trying to poison me."

Thomas Didymus looked back at him, though he might

as well have been looking away for all of the understanding in his cavern eyes.

"Withered flowers doused in gasoline," said Savior Neck. "Something wrong with springtime."

He checked his watch, jumped to his feet unsteadily, and ran back toward Main Street with a brainful of high octane.

Waste Not Want

For a small processing fee, Penny Dreadful had her fifteen minutes in the publicly accessible limelight every week. By publicly accessible I don't necessarily mean to say publicly accessed, since the only place the public could access the show was, as I've mentioned already, a public house, a tavern, a bar, the Thirteenth Step, which provided her with a maximum viewership of twenty or maybe thirty, viewership being the operative word when we recall that her listenership was pre-empted by someone dreaming a little dream from within the jukebox, unless Richie Repetition appeared on screen, in which case, as you already know, the jukebox was unplugged, wasting someone's quarter, at which time Penny Dreadful had herself an attentive, however small, viewership and listenership, meaning she wasn't entirely deluding herself when she imagined her journalism reaching an attentive, however small—small means select (let us not... oh let's not go through this again)—audience, although she might not have guessed that hardly a man—and there were only men in the Thirteenth Step—knew her by name.

And does the screen seem to be warping?

Maybe Savior Neck, Harold Esquire, Esq., Penny Dreadful, and that empty chair are a little staticky today?

Nobody in the Thirteenth Step seems to care. Nobody in the Thirteenth Step seems to notice. And don't go thinking for a second that anybody's going to waste a quarter on this one.

Introducing Violence

The following day's edition of the *Discordant Recorder* is of interest to us for two reasons: the first is on the editorial page, and the second is in the classifieds. Which isn't to say that it was at all important to the paper's general readership. No, the subscribers rarely make it beyond the funny pages, as evidenced by the way the grammar, and even the layout, falls into disrepair beyond the sports section. It's safe to assume, then, that no one but myself and Grace X. Machina, and therefore Penny Dreadful, reads past section B.

But let us not be discouraged by the apparent marginalization of our plot. Let us, for as long as is possible, delude and perhaps amuse ourselves in the manner of Penny Dreadful, by equating small numbers with selectivity, with enlightenment, and in so doing, make a heroic effort to rid ourselves of the monotonous drone of the fates, mindful of the good shepherd, who leaves the ninety-nine to go in search of the one. And having transcended points A and B, let us move on to points uncharted, unlabeled, mislabeled, giving the Discord Police Department their say and indirectly introducing violence, real violence, no more of these pratfalls and fistikatz. If the pen insists on being mightier than bare knuckles, and they wage obnoxious battle on the page, well, then, the gun will surely clear the whole mess up.

Paper, scissors, rock. (Because really, what can the paper do to the rock after the scissors have had their way with it?)

Editorial Intrusion

I maintain that I didn't waste that quarter, though I've since wished, aloud and often, that I had, as transcripts of *The Penny Dreadful Show* can cost an arm and a leg, or two arms and two legs tied with strips of a ripped up t-shirt to the bedposts, and I have to save my silver for more important practicalities and developments. And the *Discordant Recorder*? That quarter was wasted whether or not *The Penny Dreadful Show* was preempted by the jukebox: I'm no better or worse than my neighbor. I read the funny papers, too.

Only a little better or worse, as it happens, since I did manage to stumble upon a page in Section S (which, curiously, followed section C) headed: Discord P. D. Responds to Accusations. Accusations? We hadn't heard any accusations against the Discord Police Department. Precisely. Childish accusations. Seen and not heard. (Though not for lack of effort.)

No wonder they were muzzled! Effort is the enemy of progress, as evidenced by my reluctance to waste that quarter, as evidenced by the sloppy craft of the copy editors and one-hundred-proof readers. And so, to be consistent in our newfound policy, the road most taken, I present to you, unabridged and without interruption, the clipping that keeps the wheels rolling down the path of least resistance:

Discord P. D. Responds to Accusations

Their is know Officer Cats.

How the Discord Police Department had, at the time, any idea that they were accused of employing an Officer Katz is beyond me. Stranger still, imagine the editor receiving such an editorial, and puzzling over what the hell it could mean. I see him reaching for the telephone to get to the bottom of it, or at least authenticate it—it wasn't typed on department letterhead. Delivered, yes. Signed and sealed was maybe a slip of the mind—then glancing back at the page, wondering how he'll fill that column inch of space if it proves to be a forgery.

I'm also curious as to what he made of my own contribution to local journalism:

Quick, easy money. Firearm provided.
(Note the proper spelling)

Apparently only Grace X. Machina wanted quick, easy money. You expected someone bigger? stronger? hairier? I certainly did, and perhaps it would have been better that way. But, as is often the case, this placer of classified advertisements couldn't afford to be a chooser, considering the way that quarters slip through my fingers, despite my dreadful penny-pinching.

Yet, she does lend the story a sort of charm, the measure of melodrama it would have lacked had I hired, for instance, Fred Herring, head of a Main Street mercenary crew who imagine themselves mafiosi (and who, I know for a fact, thanks or no thanks to a bet he lost to Richie Repetition, looked much less elegant in a black dress).

And damn did she look elegant in black as

POINT B

sniffling occasionally, and a pair of lips whose color has by now smeared itself onto a skinny white filter. I'm an obliging host. My face falls apart too.

I play it cool. I reach up to wipe the sweat from my brow, to make sure I'm all in one piece. I'm all in one piece, and Grace X. Machina seems to have pulled herself together. I feel a nagging need to triple-check the calendar for some indication that Grace X. Machina does not in fact have the only appointment, that she's not here for the quick, easy money.

It isn't so much that she's a woman, a beautiful woman—the femme fatale is almost as common a trope as the gorilla-sized goon in a rayon suit—it's the beautiful woman that she is, disappearing and reappearing, making me do the same. She could bring my plot to a halt, leave me running in circles.

No need to check the calendar. I know what it says. But in this case the path of least resistance is a path of significant resistance because there's no other path either less or more resistant. And I'll be damned if I don't need a drink. She'll wait up here for me.

"I'll wait here," she says.

Good. You wait here.

The Rats is the Maze

Downstairs in the Thirteenth Step, I'm sitting at my table in the corner opposite the television and nursing a glass of the usual when Fred Herring stumbles in wearing a black dress and stiletto heels, and asks me for a date.

"You wanna go out with me?" says Fred Herring.

He's blocking my view of the silent screen.

But we're out, Fred Herring. Two gentlemen, despite your unfortunate attire, passing a pleasant evening at their gentlemen's club. So why stand on formality? Why stand on those enormous heels? Take off your hat, that is, your wig, have a seat, and for the love of God, get out of the way of the screen.

There are two ways to handle a situation like this: delicacy and its opposite, and there are any number of opposites. What we're really dealing with is an age-old social/philosophical debate: immediate gratification versus packing rats; pump-priming versus praying for rain, to mix a number of metaphors.

Richie Repetition is a classic example of delicacy's opposite. Raised on cartoons, video games, kool-aid and crank, he couldn't help but put Fred Herring in a tragically tight-fitting black dress and push him into the Thirteenth Step to ask for a date. Then again, Richie Repetition is living fast (on speed), will die young (and soon), and leave a particularly messy corpse regardless of whether I choose delicacy or the opposite of delicacy. How else to draw the public consciousness to the conviction of Savior Neck? The real question, then, is who does the dirty work: me or the poetry?

I'm not averse to rolling the dice when the table's in my head. That's the extent to which I'm a gambling man. Delicacy, then, if he joins me in not blocking my view of the television; the opposite for the opposite. Of course, Fred Herring has been sitting beside me ever since I offered him a seat, and I've been tipping toes on egg shells ever since, which means: a sip of the usual, eyes on the screen, never a glance at my date.

May I buy you a drink, Fred Herring, and may I call you Fred Herring? Yes, Fred Herring, a glass of the usual will make the evening a little less painful, a few might have made it enjoyable if you'd chosen a more appropriate dress. Spring is nearly upon us and black doesn't do justice to the budding leaves and the smell of freshly mown lawns. It just isn't your color, Fred Herring, but mistakes are mistakes and I've vowed to be delicate, and all of this delicacy is making me thirsty. Another drink it is. A drink it will be. The usual.

Not a glance. Perhaps a glance. And then a full-blown stare at my bigger, stronger, hairier date.

Drink up, Fred Herring, for the night is young and I will soon be taking advantage of you, very, very delicately. Unless, that is, you want your pretty mug, atop that unfortunate getup, to grace the set of *The Penny Dreadful Show*. My hand is the camera, my baby blues the lens, my head is...

The Penny Dreadful Show arrives with all of the fanfare that entails on a night without repetition. Someone within the jukebox dreams a little dream that floats beside the ghosts of cigarettes and beer-smells out the open front door and into the mellow night. Fred Herring notices my eyes on a trembling Savior Neck without noticing a trembling Savior Neck himself.

"What? Is Richie on?" says Fred Herring.

A commotion runs through the bar. The jukebox is unplugged and its dreeoommuunngg ceases as a gentle tide of whispered richies breaks toward the television in the corner.

"...joined tonight by Officer..." is all Penny Dreadful manages to say before the dreaming begins anew and the collective glare of thirty old men bears down on my date and me.

No, Fred Herring. No Richie Repetition. Not tonight. Tonight it's just me and you and a silent teevee, and damn all these old farts with their watery pink eyes. Besides, we have so much catching up to do. I haven't seen you in ages, and I don't think I ever knew about your predilection for evening-wear.

"You didn't know because it wasn't so," says Fred Herring.

A sip of the usual. Eyes on the screen. Officer Longarm looks a bit worked up, doesn't he? I'd bet he's been yelling since I'm not a gambling man.

But now it is?

Savior Neck appears to be choking. I seem to have missed something. Perhaps I was glancing at my date?

"Now what is?" says Fred Herring. I can feel him staring at me out of the corner of my eye.

Savior Neck is on the ground, on his back, convulsing. Penny Dreadful appears to be attending to him while Harold Esquire, Esq. pushes Officer Longarm away from him. Suddenly the scene is replaced by a black screen with low-tech computer-green lettering informing me that our local cable-access station is experiencing technical difficulties—Savior Neck has short-circuited—and that I should please stand by.

Now what are the odds I'll stand by? What are the odds that I could stand by with this bigger, stronger, hairier man in a dress sitting beside me? What excuse do I have now for not glancing his way? I steal a glance, then a full-blown stare at my full-grown date in his tight little dress.

Now it is so.

"No it ain't," says Fred Herring.

Now it is or my eyes deceive me. Now it is or I'm imagining those furry flabcakes bulging from your spaghetti straps. Do us both a favor, Fred Herring, and don't attempt to cast doubt on the things you truly do do. Such tactics may work with whomever you're accustomed to consorting, but try to remember that I wear the pants in this relationship.

"I wear pants," says Fred Herring.

I look at him. I look at him with all the cool of a predator who's found some sitting-still prey. He looks down at himself with the meekness of a lamb who doesn't want the lion lying with him.

"This old thing," he says, playing the coquette, "I'm only wearing this cause I lost a bet with Richie Repetition."

Is it any wonder that I'm not a gambling man? I'm not just referring to your predicament, Fred Herring, but also to Richie Repetition's. Yes, Richie Repetition, the speedfreak notorious for petty thievery and assault.

Fred Herring pretends he doesn't know what the hell I'm talking about.

"I don't know what the hell you're talking about," says Fred Herring.

Oh, I'm sure it's the same guy, positively sure. Richie Repetition. Deals speed in the neighborhood. You can't miss him. Wiry little guy, always jumpy.

Fred Herring feigns ignorance.

"I feign ignorance," says Fred Herring.

As Fred Herring feigns ignorance, Penny Dreadful gets another chance to feign journalism, and Harold Esquire, Esq. legalism, while Officer Longarm publicly relates until he's blue in the face. Savior Neck is nowhere to be seen.

You know, Fred Herring. You know who I'm talking

about. Richie Repetition. Richie Repetition who deals speed on the corner. Right outside. Right outside the Thirteenth...

"I know who Richie Repetition is," says Fred Herring. "You know I know who Richie Repetition is."

Of course I know you know who Richie Repetition is. Isn't that what I've been saying?

"I'm only here 'cause I lost a bet to him," says Fred Herring.

Now that isn't nice, Fred Herring. That's no way to treat a first date, much less a first date who only accepted this date in order to be charitable, in order to get you out of the way of the teevee.

Harold Esquire, Esq. is gesticulating wildly again. Penny Dreadful listens attentively. Officer Longarm looks like he may soon erupt.

"But I don't know anything else," says Fred Herring. "I feign ignorance to everything else you're saying and I'm not gonna let your fancy talk trick me into saying anything that I don't know nothing about."

All right, all right, Fred Herring. We'll just stop it already. Only... only... I'm so tired of this that I can hardly manage the poetry; I can hardly bring myself to pretend to care while pretending not to care; things are, things might be, I admit I haven't been concentrating—so much more interesting on teevee—but I'm a firm believer in the old finish-what-you-started school of thought with a minor in no-turning-back-now only, I thought you knew Richie Repetition better than that, Fred Herring. I thought, well I suppose it was only a suspicion, but a suspicion supported by rumor, that he might have been an associate, a business associate, a subordinate of yours.

Savior Neck returns to the set, but I can't pay attention to the television now. I'll miss seeing Fred Herring looking at me out of the corner of his eye out of the corner of my eye.

A look that seems to be saying I'm listening. Yes I want to know a secret. Closer. You can whisper in my ear.

I turn in my chair to face Fred Herring's profile. I get closer. He jumps back. Perhaps I was distracted by the jukebox.

Take it easy, Fred Herring. I was trying to whisper in your ear. I didn't think you'd want me talking business, your business, out loud. Have it your way. Now where was I? A subordinate of yours. Yes, a subordinate of yours. A subordinate of yours who manages to lose a lot of inventory.

"Lose ain't the word," says Fred Herring.

Naturally, you're right, Fred Herring, and I couldn't have said it better myself: Lose ain't the word. Indeed, lose ain't the word. Would misplace be more appropriate?

He's looking at me again out of the corner of his eye, but I won't risk getting any closer and whispering in his ear.

Do you know about the rats, Fred Herring? Of course you know about the rats.

"Are you calling me a rat?" says Fred Herring.

Patience, patience. I'm not calling you anything. I'm not calling you anything but Fred Herring. I thought we'd already covered this. Would you rather I called you something else, Mr. Herring? Would you rather I called you darling, dearest? It seems that dress is constricting your circulation. Is it at all possible that you could be this stupid in your habitual poly/rayon blends? Forgive me, forgive me, Ms. Herring. Or had we decided on darling, dearest. Or was it finally rat?

"..."

Because I could call you rat, if that's what you wanted, though I suppose I'd have to alter my metaphor.

"..."

Well then, if it's all the same to you I'm going to stick with Fred Herring. Path of least resistance, you know. Any more complicated and we'll be like rats in a maze. But the rats in the maze are of no concern to us. Of little concern to us. The rats in the maze are searching frantically for the cheese we've placed at the end. An expendable piece of cheese. In a sense, we're almost rooting for the rats in the maze, sighing when they turn in to a dead-end alley even though they don't understand our words or gestures. They only understand their sense of smell, their hunger. It's amusing how far they can be from the straight and narrow—the one and only path—and yet so close to the cheese. It's obviously a game when the rats are in the maze.

But what really concerns us are the rats who aren't in the maze, Fred Herring. What concerns us are the rats in our houses, so to speak. The rats in our houses are after more than just a crumb of cheese. The rats in our houses will take anything we leave out. They're after our dinner. They're after our bread and butter. Now why should we bother to bring home the bacon when we know the rats are only going to nibble it up? How do we keep the rats who aren't in the maze from eating, not just the expendable cheese, but the bread, butter, and bacon?

"Rat trap," says Fred Herring.

Rat traps are messy, Fred Herring. Rat traps leave trapped rats behind refrigerators, in dark cabinet corners, and in closets beneath collections of pretty dresses. If you're not in the room when the rat trap snaps, you don't even realize you have a trapped rat until the trapped-rat smell makes your nose hairs tingle. Then you have a rat corpse to take care of, and God forbid the police, or someone who might be inclined to inform the police...

"A rat," says Fred Herring.

...should catch you disposing of the rat corpse.

"So what am I supposed to do about my rat problem?" says Fred Herring.

What indeed, Fred Herring. You have to break it all down into fragments. What is your rat problem?

"…"

Is it a rat?

"It's a rat," says Fred Herring.

No, no, no, Fred Herring! Your problem is not a rat. A rat is your problem. There are many many rats in the world that are rats but not your problem.

"…"

Then is it something the rat is doing, Fred Herring? Is your rat problem something the rat is doing?

"Yeah?" says Fred Herring

Of course it is, Fred Herring. And what's it doing?

"…"

Is it losing something?

"No, I'm losing something," says Fred Herring.

And what are you losing, Fred Herring?

"My bread and butter and bacon," says Fred Herring.

And who's misplacing, who's taking the bread, the butter, the bacon that you're losing, Fred Herring?

"That rat," says Fred Herring, rushing out of the bar, as someone else says, "Richie's on," and the other old men, wary of another false alarm, react slowly so that by the time the dreeoomung ceases once again, and the volume on the television is turned up, all that's left of the commercial is, "Harold Esquire, Esq. solved all of my legal troubles," followed immediately by Thomas Didymus' declaration that he, too, is condemned to death. No one notices that they don't understand a word he says because no one pays him any attention.

The Rats in Our Houses

Grace X. Machina has been waiting for me. In my office, above the Thirteenth Step. She has an appointment, and with the bigger, stronger, hairier Fred Herring frying the fish, at no cost to me, of what he sees as his own rat problem, I feel confident she'll have no trouble earning some quick, easy money with the firearm that I provide.

I provide her with a firearm, a revolver, though it may as well be a blunderbuss for all I know about guns. It was lent to me by Vinnie Domino, over-the-counter from under-the-counter, illegally, I assume. It's fully loaded, one bullet in each of the six chambers. I can't imagine needing any more. I can't imagine my needing any at all. I can't even bring myself to touch it without a handkerchief between my lily-white hands and its textured steel grip. I am, after all, little more than a bureaucrat, just taking care of the paperwork. Leave the rest up to the hired guns, the hired hands that fire the borrowed guns, Grace out of the machine and into my machinations, a well-paid pawn. Note the proper spelling.

"My name is Grace X. Machina," says Grace X. Machina, examining the firearm, turning it about in her hands. "I believe we had an appointment."

Our appointment is nearly over, Grace X. Machina. The firearm has been provided. The money is quick and easy, but not so quick and easy that I can afford to pay you for taking a firearm. No, the firearm is your advance and your expense account. I won't be needing a receipt.

I hand her a slip of paper, her instructions.

Now hurry, Grace X. Machina. Our appointment is over

and you must move quickly to the next.

Grace X. Machina appears to be confused. She looks at me, at the gun in her hand, at the slip of paper—as slip of paper rather than instructions—at me. I hand her my hand. She looks at my hand, stands up, walks out the door.

Forgiveness

It's a curious breed of unambitious characters that scuttles in and out of Discord, a curiously unambitious breed, and I find it difficult to fault myself for this. And I don't find it difficult to fault them. Take, for instance, since she's likely to be freshest in memory, Grace X. Machina. Now, it isn't perfectly reasonable for a potential employer to expect that a potential employee will become an actual employee, given the opportunity. It isn't unreasonable to expect this. In fact, if the potential employer is worth a damn as a student of human behavior, it may even be reasonable. But it can never be perfectly reasonable. Not in this market. In this market the employee's always right, even if the employee is only a potential employee, and her rightness as a potential employee lies in deciding not to accept my offer of employment.

If this were the whole of it, then I wouldn't find it difficult to fault myself, and I would fault myself even if I did. But this isn't the whole of it.

The whole of it must take into account that I don't own a gun, that I needed a gun so I borrowed a gun, with every intention of returning the gun to the rightful owner of the gun after using the gun, and, if necessary, replenishing it with ammunition.

The whole of it must take into account that the gun was initially to be used for purposes that it isn't being used for, purposes of intimidation, even personal harm if the need arose, purposes leading to purposes leading to purposes.

The whole of it must take into account that even now, Penny Dreadful is across the hall in her office clack-clacking away at her typewriter, clack-clacking away at a purpose that remains an enigma to me for lack of ambition, a gun, three dollars plus shipping and handling.

And if I do have three dollars? Ladies and gentlemen, there are, there always will be matters of principle. There must be. How many times should I mail my check or money order for three dollars plus shipping and handling only to find that my transcript hasn't been shipped and handled, or hasn't been shipped and handled properly? Seventy times seven? Then let this be the four hundred ninety-first. And let me take this one by force.

Yet it doesn't seem like I'll be taking this one at all, either by force or fee, because Penny Dreadful is still in her office, clack-clacking away.

I heard Grace X. Machina's heels click-clicking across the hall. I heard her knock on Penny Dreadful's door. I heard Penny Dreadful answer the door, but I didn't hear any intimidation or personal harm. Then I heard Penny Dreadful's door shut. I heard Grace X. Machina click-clicking down the hall toward the stairs, and when I came out to remind her of her instructions, I found a crumpled slip of paper on the floor outside my door, reading:

Go directly across the hall and obtain a copy of the most recent episode of the Penny Dreadful Show

USE ANY NECESSARY MEANS!

Still, I should set aside the three dollars, along with the rest of the quick, easy money, in case Grace X. Machina stumbles into some sense.

The Usual Unusual

Grace X. Machina stumbles at the foot of the stairs and is helped to her feet by many old men who weren't here when she arrived for our appointment, and are surprised to find such a beautiful woman, any woman at all actually, besides Fred Herring, who's already at home, in their watering hole.

The Thirteenth Step is full now, as full as it gets, and all the old men are lining up to buy her drinks. Grace X. Machina, whom we already know to be obliging if noncommittal, accepts them, the drinks, one after another, putting them down as quickly as Vinnie Domino can set them up, always a hand on her heavy handbag.

The men are grateful she's willing to drink her fill on their bill, and though they see that she's a bit high-strung and probably nervous, clutching her handbag tightly as though it could protect her from any among them who would attempt to earn a higher return on his investment, they're happy spending an evening spending earnings on drinks they don't have to drink. So happy, in fact, that the jukebox is allowed to play itself out, though the television remains staticky-silent, and the only sounds are the gulp of her gullet, the clock of empty glass on hardwood, and the oooo's and aaaaaaahhhhh's of the old men, first at her beauty, and eventually at her capacity, until she's drunk a drink on every man in the house.

At which point she leaves the house, heavy hand on bag, standing and walking on those heels as steadily as if she'd been drinking water the whole time, perhaps more, since she doesn't stumble at all, click-clicking directionless down Main Street, fully loaded.

Gauche

In his newfound sobriety, Savior Neck took to spending time beneath the overpass with Thomas Didymus and his can of gasoline. See him there, face over the nozzle, coping with his death sentence without the inkling of a suspicion of how very soon his life will be over.

Like a snapshot from the buddy collage in the senior annual of a school from which no one ever manages to graduate, Savior Neck and Thomas Didymus, frozen in black and white:

Savior Neck: This is the smell of my own death.

Thomas Didymus: ...

They never did have much to say to each other. You've heard it all before.

I only wish there was something I could do to make his last days in Discord a bit more pleasurable, more interesting—a vacation, maybe, or a going-away party—but I don't have the time to care for him as is, leaving him a sort of latchkey kid, Thomas Didymus his babysitter, doing what they do when they find the liquor cabinet locked in a house the size of a small city.

And it's a small city after all, because here comes the drunk but not disorderly Grace X. Machina, striding toward the two boys and their can of gasoline, as though she meant to be striding toward them, as though the space beneath a highway overpass where two men are inhaling gasoline fumes from a can were a conventional destination for a woman and her gun after an evening heavy with drink.

God, providence, whatever you may call it, working in

mysterious ways seems such a tired cliché until God, providence, whatever you may call it begins working in mysterious ways, at which point you can only sit back and watch the tangled web weave itself. I've been trying now for so long to unite Grace X. Machina, a gun, and these boys, that I'm briefly humbled by Grace X. Machina's liquid intuition, if that's what it is. Cut out the middle woman and no need for pinching pennies. Truly the path of least resistance is no path at all, but stasis, points A and B resting intertwined, each atop the other, depending on which way you spin it. And I had only to recognize their stasis for their stasis to be. (I'm crying as I pen these words.)

Of course, there's a difference between the proximity of Grace X. Machina to the gun to the boys, and the proper utilization of the gun to properly kill whoever of them is truly condemned to death (this too we will leave up to fate) and end his death sentence. Contiguity does not imply causality, and I'm so tired of being the cause, no matter how proper my utilization. So for now and if only forever, I'll leave these things to the grace of God and follow my Grace X. Machina to her seat at the right hand of Savior Neck, who is in turn seated at the right hand of Thomas Didymus, who is, you remember, left-handed. Sinister.

For a moment, for several, there was silence save for the rumble of the occasional truck passing over them. The occasional truck stirred up the occasional road grit that coated Thomas Didymus and Savior Neck in a fine gray dust streaked with black. The occasional grit was occasional enough that the two regulars had either grown accustomed to it or come to appreciate it as a hallmark of the beneath-the-overpass experience. The newcomer, on the other hand, was unaware there was experience to be had, so when she experienced the fall of the occasional grit onto her fashionable clothing and onto her skin and into her nose and mouth, it became an occasion for coughing and gagging and spitting.

Grace X. Machina coughs and gags and spits, stands, coughs and gags and spits. Thomas Didymus and Savior Neck look like statues in the dust-coated darkness, and it looks like the statues are looking at Grace X. Machina as she coughs and gags and spits.

But these days, they not only look like statues, they seem to move as slowly too. They don't bother to offer her any assistance—a pat on the back, a glass of water—because they know by the time either of them could stand up and move toward her, much less find a glass of water, Grace X. Machina will be through with her coughing and gagging and spitting.

When Grace X. Machina is through, she doesn't sit down again at the right hand of Savior Neck. She spits one last time, lights a cigarette, coughs one last time.

Slowly, with both hands, Savior Neck offers the can of gasoline to Grace X. Machina. Grace X. Machina responds by puffing a cloud of smoke in his direction. Thomas Didymus, who, like his twin, has taken to wearing a withered flower doused in gasoline in his lapel, takes the withered flower from his lapel, and offers it to Grace X. Machina, slowly, with his left hand. Grace X. Machina accepts it, and sits down beside Thomas Didymus, sniffing at the flower.

Savior Neck feels the emptiness in the space beside him, an emptiness that wasn't an emptiness before it was occupied, an emptiness that isn't filled by the can of gasoline placed there for lack of anything more to do with it, can or space. It's an emptiness that can be taken for granted, but not forgotten, an emptiness that bends his back forward and turns his head left, that forces him to watch Grace X. Machina sniff her flower, to watch her savor the smell of his own death.

"That," says Savior Neck, "is the smell of my death."

She puffs a cloud of smoke in his direction. Thomas Didymus and Grace X. Machina gradually dissolve, the smoke filling in the empty space between the space of Thomas Didymus and the space of Savior Neck. He can't see them, they won't see him. But he knows they're there.

"The smell of a withered flower doused in gasoline," says Savior Neck. "That's what I mean."

The smoke stirs but still no sight. Savior Neck sits awhile, awaiting a response that doesn't arrive. The emptiness grows, surrounding him, pushing his back against the stone wall of the overpass, turning his head right, where there's also smoke.

"It's something I think about a lot," says Savior Neck. "Being I'm condemned to death. I feel like maybe I know what it smells like. Death, I mean."

The smoke is still, the scene is still, and the silence sounds like death, and Savior Neck continues to soliloquize.

"He's condemned to death too. Not just me. But I was condemned to death first, so I've had more time to think about it. I guess it's my cross to bear, this conviction. Just don't know when it's gonna happen. That's the worst part. They already tried a couple times, but..."

The occasional truck passes over, stirring up the occasional grit, but Grace X. Machina doesn't cough, gag or spit. Savior Neck continues soliloquizing until he's soliloquized himself to sleep.

simplicity

I feel as if I've been negligent, almost malicious, in the way I've handled the Shirley Goodness Retirement Paradise. We've come this far, and still I've given very little in the way of real information, hard data. But the path of least resistance seems to be circular, since it's brought us here again, and it would be sadistic of me—bureaucrats often have a sadistic streak—to leave you in the dark.

But I'll leave Thomas Didymus and Grace X. Machina in the dark. The Shirley Goodness Retirement Paradise hasn't seen electric light—save for the occasional beam from the flashlight of one of the more spelunkish children, and there are a few in every generation, or the occasional beam from the flashlight of one of the more diligent police officers, Officer Longarm, for instance, picking through squatters and belongings and the bodies and belongings of former squatters, expecting to find God knows what—in years.

But Thomas Didymus and Grace X. Machina don't have a flashlight; they have Grace X. Machina's matches, and they aren't looking for squatters, they're looking to squat. Matches, though, are deceitful and ephemeral. Strike one. It lights the room suddenly, uncertainly, like a two-dimensional canvas by a too-dramatic painter, and, just as suddenly, it singes your fingers, is dropped to the floor.

A dropped match will usually extinguish itself by the time it hits the ground, or whatever may be on the ground—paper, pipes, a person—that you didn't have time to notice, or didn't notice because your feet remained in shadows, but the Shirley Goodness Retirement Paradise is a major fire hazard. It was a fire hazard well before the fire that killed the parents of Discord's parents and abandoned it to a lower-rent generation. Which isn't to say that any of Grace X. Machina's matches have ignited, or will ignite any blazes.

I suppose my guilty conscience in this case comes from my failure to indicate that the Shirley Goodness Retirement Paradise is a bit more discordant than the rest of Discord. It was abandoned before Discord was abandoned. Its bones are brittling and breaking more quickly than the city's other brittle bones, its drafts are draftier, its windows shattereder and boardeder, the holes in the floors more holy than any in the city, and it will be officially demolished long before Discord returns to the dust from whence it came.

But now I'm being too generous, and generosity, unfortunately, will kill neither the cat nor the rat nor anyone else. The dying must begin soon or we'll find ourselves, like the parents of Discord's parents, trapped on the top floor of a relatively towering inferno without the means to exit gracefully or mostly at all.

Gracefully, though, doesn't apply here, not now that the effects of the alcohol are beginning to wear off. Grace X. Machina is reverting to clumsiness, not as a matter of choice but as a matter of fact she's tripping upstairs and falling on flat ground.

Thomas Didymus isn't helping matters any. He has a peculiarly unsubtle way of bumping into Grace X. Machina. Actually, the bumping into Grace X. Machina is only a by-product of his bumping into Grace X. Machina's heavy handbag. He'd noticed something about the way she'd stridden toward him and whatsisname and their gas can, as though the space beneath a highway overpass where two filthy men are inhaling gasoline fumes from a can were the conventional destination of a woman and... and what? Something about her confidence, her grace

"I just realized you don't even know my name," says Grace X. Machina.

Thomas Didymus brushes against her hand on her handbag, knocking her sideways, down a step, her other hand gripping the surprisingly-still-solid railing as her body arches backward. There is grace in this curve despite her clumsiness and his clumsiness.

Yes, the effects of the alcohol on Grace X. Machina are beginning to wear off, but the effects of the gasoline on Thomas Didymus are of a more permanent nature. He's still moving as slowly as ever, so he doesn't move to help her, and her graceful arc lasts longer than might be expected.

Thomas Didymus' slow-motion mind is still assessing the situation. Above him, the room he calls home when he etc. Beside him, the statue of a dark woman in a dress teetering on a dark step, clutching her heavy handbag in one hand, the railing in the other. But there was something else, something that came before the fall...

The brain is a simple creature crammed into the skull of a simple creature. I'm referring specifically to Thomas Didymus, though not only to Thomas Didymus. But Thomas Didymus' brain, which has taken a long and systematic beating beneath the fists of the fumes, thinks simplistically, and it doesn't wish to think two thoughts at once, and the brain will move all the more slowly when forced to remember two things or any number of things added to one thing, even unto paralysis.

The body, though, doesn't necessarily work in conjunction with the brain. I'm referring specifically though not only to Thomas Didymus. Witness Grace X. Machina's extended arc, which her mind would surely work to change if her mind could work to change it.

Apparently Thomas Didymus' mouth remembers what his brain doesn't, because his mouth says, "It's probably better that way."

"It's probably better that way it's probably better that way," over and over his mouth repeats, "it's probably better that way," desperate that its brain should understand.

But I can only wish luck to the brain that hopes to understand what Thomas Didymus' mouth is saying since gasoline affects the tongue as it affects the rest of the body and the mind, and the fumes also roll from between his lips. His very breath is fumes.

"It's probably better that way it's probably better that way," says Thomas Didymus' mouth to his frozen-over brain, answering Grace X. Machina's statement, though Grace X. Machina hears only sounds I can't print, not for lack of sense but for lack of syllables in this in the beginning was the world of ours, a shrieking, laughing, groaning cry of anonymous, lifeless, deathless, languageless on and onnity that terrifies poor Grace X. Machina straight over the surprisingly-still-strong railing, stupid, stupid bodies, involuntarily reacting into dangling down a stairwell by one arm the other clutching heavy handbag all of the above clutched and clawed at by the gravity of the situation pulls stiletto heels down down away from their feet into shadows then blackness.

Click one. Click another. Echoing up the empty.

"Give me your hand," says Thomas Didymus, "give me your hand."

The hand still heavy on the handbag. Grace X. Machina's hand remains heavy on its handbag and her ears hear only the terror of Thomas Didymus' tongue.

"Your hand, your hand," he says, his body tapping into a reserve of energy that I wasn't aware existed, trying to pry her hand, finger by finger, from the railing, to pull her up over the railing to the relative safety of the steps.

Grace X. Machina struggles against his trying to save her to save herself. He pulls one finger from the railing, moves to the next, and she clenches the railing more tightly with the one just pried. Meanwhile, she reaches into her handbag, pulls the gun, and gives Thomas Didymus exactly what they wanted all along.

As Thomas Didymus was going bang

Savior Neck was dreaming a little dream of me. Well, I was there. But then, so was everyone else, everyone else who was in on it.

Asleep beneath the overpass, Savior Neck dreamed he woke up, as Officer Longarm drove up, to find that the smoke had cleared away along with Thomas Didymus and Grace X. Machina.

It was no longer winter, or it was on the verge of being no longer winter. The night was particularly mellow for Discord on the verge of being no longer winter, and Savior Neck was in no particular danger, no danger at the hands of the elements, but still, there were Officer Longarm and his partner, idling in front of Savior Neck as though in the midst of a blizzard, as though the encounter wasn't pure serendipity, as though there was a reason for them to be idling there in front of Savior Neck.

"What brings you out here this time of night?" said Officer Longarm, as though it wasn't perfectly obvious, even without a glance at the can of gasoline beside him.

Savior Neck's eyes met Officer Longarm's motionless, but he didn't respond.

It isn't a question of whether he would have engaged Officer Longarm in idle chat, but whether he could have. By then, Savior Neck had spent a good deal of time beneath the overpass with Thomas Didymus and his can of gasoline. Whether it was time enough to bring the brainworks to a halt I can't say. Besides, this is a dream, and who knows what language he speaks in dreams.

For our purposes, they spoke English in Savior Neck's dream.

"Get in the car," said Officer Longarm's partner, with an edge of disappointment in his voice, disappointment in Savior Neck for deciding or not deciding not to play their little game again.

Or was it apprehension at the possibility of another messy birth? Game or no game, disappointment or apprehension, the officers had a strong sense of duty. A strong sense of duty to whom? Who calls the shots in Savior Neck's dream? Obviously not Savior Neck. He followed his own sense of duty, or fate, slowly, gasoline slowly, so slowly that the officers became impatient, into the back seat without questions and without answers.

They cruised quietly through the streets, Savior Neck staring out the window as though into his own eyelids, Officer Longarm sniffing at the stench of gasoline, his partner driving, just as dawn was sneaking into Discord, stretching pinkly after a too-long night's sleep, brushing the gray from its eyes and holding the sun up to show the city much the same in appearance as it had been when it had gone to bed—dingy cracked and empty. The car stopped in front of the Shirley Goodness Retirement Paradise and Officer Longarm's partner told Savior Neck to get out.

"Get out," said Officer Longarm's partner.

But he didn't get the chance to. Officer Longarm's partner himself got out, went around the car, opened Savior Neck's door, and lifted him out of the seat before he had even processed the order. He set Savior Neck on the ground almost gently and dusted himself off. Savior Neck, too, dusted his dusty self, slowly, and to no avail. The officers sped away, relieved they wouldn't be spending the rest of their shift wiping piss from the back seat, before Savior Neck even got to his feet.

The sun slowly climbed the sky, but Savior Neck didn't see it, because he was inside the Shirley Goodness Retirement Paradise, in the stairwell, climbing just as slowly, just as steadily, without a match to light his way, stumbling over paper, pipes, people toward his high noon—back again to his father's room, the top floor. He didn't know what to expect. He climbed as though instinctively toward the only place in the building he could have been summoned to.

Pausing at the top of the floor to catch his breath, he gazed down into the darkness of staircases closing in on each other into blackness and wondered, finally, what, beyond Officer Longarm, had brought him there. Of course, it wasn't long before suspicion made its way to the top of the stairs to deliver a message from delusion, confusion, and amusement suggesting that the top floor of the Shirley Goodness Retirement Paradise was to be his final resting place, as it was his father's before him.

So he was surprised when we yelled "surprise" at his entrance. We, that is, all of us, all of us who were in on it.

"SURPRISE!" we yelled, and he was surprised backward into a wall, sliding down as slowly as ever until he reached the floor.

I was there, and so was Vinnie Domino, standing at the punch table true to type. Harold Esquire, Esq. had already had a few and was toasting Savior Neck loudly and violently, saying, "It wasn't long ago a few of us realized..." Richie Repetition was beside him, kinetic as ever, getting knocked in the head by stray gestures. Joey Katz was leaning against the wall opposite Savior Neck with a glass in his hand and the cat on his shoulder, and the cat's breath still lingered in the air before it, the rancid breath that spelled the word surprise now dissipating, but still the source of humorous comments among the guests. Savior Neck's father stood ranting at the no-good son who'd put him in this godforsaken shithole. Thomas Didymus and Grace X. Machina and her gun, the gun I borrowed from Vinnie Domino, were in the corner, lost in their own cloud of smoke. In fact, I'm not even sure those two said "surprise." Then there was Penny Dreadful, documenting the whole thing with a camera.

Harold Esquire, Esq. finished his toast and everyone agreed "here here" and sipped or gulped from their drinks—or didn't notice there'd been a toast in the case of Thomas Didymus and Grace X. Machina, or didn't have a glass to sip from like Savior Neck—then there was a pause, the awkward silence of some who don't know what to do next and others who don't know or care how to go about what to do next.

It was supposed to be Grace X. Machina. She had the gun. But she also had someone, and that someone was taking her attention away from someone else to whom common decency dictated she should have been attending. Common decency and the prospect of quick, easy money. Even in Savior Neck's dream Grace X. Machina lacks ambition. Even in Savior Neck's dream they're a curious breed of characters. Even in Savior Neck's dream Savior Neck refuses to realize I want nothing but to remind him that he's alive.

Maybe this wrecking ball will help.

A wrecking ball smashes sidewise across the room, taking me, taking everyone else who was in on it along with it, taking the whole Shirley Goodness Retirement Paradise with it, the whole city of Discord, the whole phenomenal world with it, leaving Savior Neck alone and unharmed to enjoy the life I only threatened in order to remind him that it was there.

As Thomas Didymus was going bang, and Savior Neck was dreaming a little dream

I was in the Thirteenth Step clocking glass after glass of the usual against the bar and dodging Vinnie Domino's questions about the whereabouts of his gun, the whenabouts he would be getting it back, the whatabouts I was doing with it in the first place.

Killing, of course, though I'm not killing directly and Grace X. Machina isn't killing the people I wanted dead in the order I had intended, though Thomas Didymus would have had to go sooner or later, thanks to his completely self-imposed death sentence.

But I was dodging Vinnie Domino's questions, so I didn't answer killing, though what else one might do with a borrowed gun is beyond me...

Ladies' night at the firing range, I say.

"But you aren't a lady," says Vinnie Domino.

Please don't let us go through this twice in one night. Even a good farce is tiresome if it continues once it's over and this farce is over and it's not a good farce.

As Thomas Didymus was going bang and Savior Neck was dreaming a little dream and I was clocking glasses on the bar

Harold Esquire, Esq. was in the hallway above the Thirteenth Step, knock-knock-knocking on Penny's door. He held a bouquet of flowers in the hand that wasn't knock-knock-knocking. Penny Dreadful didn't feel obliged to who's-there. She kept clack-clack-clacking away with a purpose that must remain an enigma to me. It seems they'd had a little tiff over Penny Dreadful's journalistic integrity—she wouldn't reveal her source, who wasn't so much a source as a cause of news. The same issue that had gotten her fired from her old job in Cincinnati and forced her to return to Discord—using a source as cause. And who is my source? My cause.

As Thomas Didymus was going bang and Savior Neck was dreaming a little dream and I was clocking glasses on the bar and Harold Esquire, Esq. was knock-knock-knocking on Penny's door and Penny Dreadful was clack-clacking away

Fred Herring, sans dress, avec pajamas, surprisingly domestic flannel pajamas, was listening to the snap-snap of rat traps with a deep satisfaction. Poison, I'd told him, not traps, but what fucking difference does it make when I wasn't talking about rats in the first place. A curious breed, a curiously unambitious breed.

As Thomas Didymus was going bang and Savior Neck was dreaming a little dream and I was clocking glasses on the bar and Penny Dreadful was clack-clacking away and Harold Esquire, Esq. was knock-knock-knocking on Penny's door and Fred Herring was listening to the snap-snap of rat traps with a deep satisfaction...

First I should point out that Thomas Didymus exploded. Yes, he got shot, but then he exploded. The boy's heart pumped petrol. Now his ventricles, pieces of his ventricles, and all the rest of his pieces are flying toward all points of the compass, moving far more quickly than they ever did when he was alive. And as pieces of him were flying away from their center, whatever or wherever that was, and out toward the walls of the stairwell and down toward dangling Grace X. Machina and farther down toward and into the shadows then blackness where Grace X. Machina's shoes have ceased their click-clicking; as pieces of him fly up the stairs toward the top floor, toward the room as four bare walls that Thomas Didymus used to call home, these flying Didymi are licked at by tongues of flame which are devoured by gaping mouths of flame which are swallowed by throats of flame and so on and so forth. Add to this exploding the incessant screams of Grace X. Machina and you can be sure it wasn't a quiet time in the usually pin-drop-echoes-off-the-static-walls of the Shirley Goodness Retirement Paradise.

I should also mention that there was a reason Thomas Didymus, an old-looking young man who spent most of his time beneath a highway overpass inhaling gasoline fumes from a can, spent most of his time beneath a highway overpass (feel free to assume that there's also a reason for his inhaling gasoline fumes, but be aware that I'm no psychologist, and the odds are against your being one, and that much of this mess is a direct or directly traceable result of my failed attempts at playing psychologist. Bureaucrats should stick to pushing pencils): Richie Repetition, the local speedfreak, notorious for petty thievery and assault, made his home on the same floor of the same building that Thomas Didymus called home when he cared to call something home.

If there's one thing that my time in Discord has taught me, and I'm as aware as you are of my recent rant against head-shrinking, it's that received wisdom isn't always wise, especially this particular piece of received wisdom: a gentle word turneth away anger.

A gentle word does not turneth away anger. A gentle word multiplies wrath tenfold or some such abstract multiplication of an already abstract measurement, and Thomas Didymus, is, was, always gentle despite impediments to his speech and despite anything that Grace X. Machina might have to say, and Richie Repetition is always angry.

Richie Repetition is angered by the explosion and screaming sounds issuing from the stairwell. First he is awakened by them and then he is angered by them or he is always angry and he needs only to awaken to explosion and screaming sounds to propel anger into action.

After Richie Repetition awakes, the sounds of explosion and screaming propel his anger into action, propel his body out of his room, down the hallway and into the stairwell, where he comes face to face with pieces of Thomas Didymus' face and other pieces and flames upon flames upon flames, and the pieces of body smear his body and the flames ignite on Richie Repetition's clothes and in his hair and proceed to burn Richie Repetition.

Add to the sounds of explosion and screams the surprisingly girlish screams of Richie Repetition.

Subtract from the sounds of explosion and screams the appropriately terrified screams of the still-dangling Grace X. Machina.

The sound of two screamers screaming is more than Grace X. Machina wants to contribute to. Besides, there are more pressing matters at hand, for instance, her dangling, which has been going on for several minutes now.

Richie Repetition continues to scream as Grace X. Machina tries to swing herself up and over the railing with little success. She's still dangling and swinging by only one hand, the other one gripping the gun, my gun, the one I borrowed from Vinnie Domino, as tightly as ever. After a few thrusts, she realizes the swinging isn't getting her anywhere, at least not over the railing, and she takes a moment to consider her options.

Richie Repetition is running in circles, batting at various flames on various parts of himself, screaming, while Grace X. Machina is trying to think. The sound of explosion has faded into the crackling of patches and pieces of fire scattered here and there about the stairwell, and combined with Richie Repetition's frantic antics and the echoes bouncing off the walls up and down the stairs, there's a sound of stillness, almost eerie in the midst of so much trauma.

"Can you give me a hand?" says Grace X. Machina.

Is she asking Richie Repetition? She may as well be asking Thomas Didymus for all Richie Repetition's worth to her right now.

"Stop, drop, and roll," says Grace X. Machina, but Richie Repetition has already stopped, though he hasn't stopped screaming, and dropped, lying on his back at the top of the staircase, hands over his face as his screams hoarsen then sob, thrashing from side to side—rolling is a distinct possibility.

"Now do you think you could give me a hand?" says Grace X. Machina.

I should mention that Grace X. Machina is in no wise familiar with Richie Repetition. She doesn't even recognize him from the street corner where he spends much of his time, where she, clearly, has spent none of her own, and she only had that one evening, repetition-free—can it be that it was only a few hours ago?—at the Thirteenth Step, where she might sooner or later have learned a little more about him, though the men there surely wouldn't have told her, at least not so blatantly, that Richie Repetition was not exactly the knight-in-shining-armor type.

Thomas Didymus, too, had he not found such a quick and easy, albeit messy, way to expedite his own demise, might have tried to warn her about the kind of man Richie Repetition was, since he knew firsthand, but it's unlikely she would have taken his warning, which she wouldn't have known was a warning, any more kindly than she did his attempt to save her life before he helped her to help him end his.

In any case, Richie Repetition was busy nursing his own wounds, if nursing it can be called. Crying and thrashing, he still hasn't taken any notice of Grace X. Machina, who is still dangling by one hand with a gun in the other, and who has by now called for help several more times.

There are others, ghosts and people haunting the halls of the Shirley Goodness Retirement Paradise, to whom she may be calling for help, but calling these ghosts and people from the top floor is a waste of her breath since all of them, ghosts and people, fear Richie Repetition, even a sobbing and broken Richie Repetition who may also be a broken-boned Richie Repetition now that he's fallen down the top flight of stairs to the landing where he rests like a pieta without its virgin.

Grace X. Machina watched him fall, watched him cartwheel down the stairs, and for an instant, their eyes, hers bloodshot staring upward as though still pleading for help from a stranger now obviously in a much worse position than she, his, lodged in a topsy-turvy face, surrounded by blackened skin smelling of burn, which is a smell of death, gazing glazed into hers accidentally and unaware of their own pain and fear, met, and Grace X. Machina thought that whether he was any longer in pain or not, he was no longer a threat to her safety, so she slipped the gun heavy back into her handbag, and reached for the railing with her finally free hand.

As she climbs over the railing and onto the step, she hears a consciousness-betraying groan from Richie Repetition, just a groan, the sobs having slipped farther down the stairs than his body. She pats her heavy handbag and leaves her hand there since, with her other hand now free to hold the railing in a less desperate way, that is, to guide her hand down the dark stairs, she has no other more pressing use for it.

Another groan from Richie Repetition, and some stirring. Grace X. Machina stumbles clumsily-cautious toward the sound until she's directly above it. She registers the smell of burnt flesh, which is a smell of death, and the smell of rotting breath from rotten teeth, which is a trademark smell of Richie Repetition's death, and she assumes that she's hearing and smelling him die.

She bends down, following sound and smell until she's inches from his face, where the sounds and smells are that much stronger. So much of him is already dead, it's hard to imagine him feeling any pain, but she feels his pain anyway, and there's tenderness in her as she runs her hand slowly across his face, like a body turned inside-out, raw as red to the touch, his groans now almost subtonal, hypnotic and constant.

Grace X. Machina feels Richie Repetition's misery, and it's unbearable. It's for her own sake and not his that she pulls the gun from the handbag and cocks it.

The phantom of Richie Repetition's skin still feels, senses the barrel of the gun near what is only technically now his nose. His ears hear the click of the hammer. Grace X. Machina doesn't take the time to consider whether he's begging for his life or for his death.

She pads down the stairs quickly, without stopping for her shoes and without further incident. She's almost gone before the first timid shadow, the only timid shadow bold enough, creeps into the stairwell to see for himself what has taken place.

So Joey Katz doesn't live above a bar on Main Street after all.

Dream Interpretation

Savior Neck awakes beneath the overpass to find the smoke cleared away, along with Thomas Didymus and Grace X. Machina, to find himself alone as Officer Longarm and his partner drive toward him or the space beneath the overpass in their patrol car, bumping over potholes and trailing a cloud of dust.

Overlooking further delusion and confusion and amusement over déjà vu, and quirky flirtationisms about its sense of timing, its whimsical poignancy, since there's no one around to identify with, and assuming that Savior Neck's subconscious brought its A-game, that there's no reason to include the possibility the dream symbolized falsely, then it was either a good dream or a bad dream, by which I don't mean to examine its philosophical, political, practical, or artistic merits, but whether that which the dream signified for Savior Neck was good or bad according to whom.

And, of course, it's Savior Neck about whom I'm most concerned in this case, as it's Savior Neck who isn't condemned to death, though I may very well have to kill him to prove it as I've killed others already to prove the same despite the fact that I've killed no one directly and didn't give Grace X. Machina the orders she followed.

An example of the dream signifying good for Savior Neck: Surprise! It was a big joke all along. We just thought that pretending you were condemned to death would be a good way of reminding you that you're alive.

An example of the dream signifying bad for Savior Neck: Surprise! You die alone as you have lived alone.

Notice that I didn't conjoin the two approaches, but left them both freestanding, numberless and valueless. Naturally, due to the constrictions of space-time—constrictions that exist whether randomly or specifically, whether on a network or a grid—one approach must come before the other. But this should indicate no judgment in value. In order to be fair, I pulled straws from a hat to decide which I would list first. It just happens that when there are only two straws you have a fifty-fifty chance of being right.

Savior Neck, though, would have us add a third straw, a straw that begs blatant value judgment, the straw of literal interpretation: sometimes a patrol car is just a patrol car. Value judgment: stupid. He's already standing up, readying himself for the climb into the back seat, before Officer Longarm's partner even applies the brakes.

He brakes to a stop beside Savior Neck, and Officer Longarm rolls down the passenger-side window with a grunt at the bottom of every counterclockwise cycle while Savior Neck moves slowly toward the car.

"What brings you out here this time of day?" says Officer Longarm, as though it isn't perfectly obvious, even without a glance at his can of gasoline.

Savior Neck opens the door and climbs into the back seat without answering.

"This isn't a taxi," says Officer Longarm's partner.

Savior Neck slams the door closed and folds his hands over his lap, an old prisoner reconciled to the world's impending disappearance, patiently awaiting his ride to oblivion.

"What do you think you're doing?" says Officer Longarm's partner, glancing at his obviously drunken passenger in the rearview mirror.

Savior Neck's eyes meet his, then turn toward the window. He rests his head against the glass, smudging it with grit and dust, clouding it with his breath.

"I know my rights," says Savior Neck, in his petrolect. "I may have to go with you, but I don't have to talk to you."

He touches the window with a finger, scribbles something in the fog, rubs the finger against his thumb, looks at the tip of his thumb, of his finger, and sees the skin that was hiding beneath the grime. He brings his hands to his face, spits into his palms, rubs them together.

Officer Longarm and his partner sniff the air, for alcohol or piss, but smell only dirty-man smells and gasoline smells. They watch Savior Neck and curse the fate that would bring them such a lush so early in their shift.

"Where do you think we're taking you?" says Officer Longarm.

But Savior Neck knows his rights, and he doesn't have to talk to Officer Longarm or his partner, and he isn't going to talk to them. He knows as well as they do where they're going and he doesn't have to tell and he doesn't have to be told.

They don't know where they're going, but even the most conscientious of police officers grows lazy now and again. Officer Longarm's partner puts the car in gear and drives nowhere, meaning there is no destination. To properly use a patrol car, one must by definition patrol.

The trip to the Shirley Goodness Retirement Paradise is a long and circuitous one full of twists and turns and retracing of tire tracks, for security purposes, or so Savior Neck assumes. Back toward Main Street and down a dark alley and again away from the city, all the way to the Discordant Falls.

After a few passes around the town, Officer Longarm's partner has forgotten about his passenger, and when he glances at the rearview mirror while making a left-hand turn, he's suddenly shocked by what he sees—just Savior

Neck, but enough of a surprise that he slams the brakes and is rear-ended by an unsuspecting motorist.

Nothing serious. Officer Longarm gets out to inspect the damage, to take the blame on his partner's behalf, to point to pieces of automobile and say obvious things about the pieces, like "Your headlight's broken" and "There's a little dent on the fender."

His partner grows impatient, and gets out to blame the unsuspecting motorist, to point to pieces of automobile and say unrelated and generally intimidating things, like "If I have to pay for that headlight, your head's going to get broken" and "I've made bigger dents than that with my bare fists."

Savior Neck, too, is growing impatient. Officer Longarm's partner left the car running, and the digital-green clock on the dash indicates that it's nearing noon, and though Savior Neck has only just noticed the clock, which means he doesn't know exactly how long it's been since the officers got out, he's sure it's already taken longer than it should have with still no sign of an end to the fender-bender summit.

He's old and he's slow, and you'll remember that he's never driven a car, but somehow he manages to climb into the front seat, situate himself behind the wheel, and drive off before the officers and Joey Katz—who was returning to the Shirley Goodness Retirement Paradise from the Thirteenth Step, where he'd just delivered some interesting news that he didn't even have to cause—have time to notice, much less do anything about.

Zero

I'm asleep at my desk when Grace X. Machina enters my office through a cloud of smoke from her long, skinny cigarette. She doesn't have an appointment—I don't have to check my desk calendar to know that—but she does have a number of injuries—deep burns on her pretty face and arms, smears of blood, whether hers or Thomas Didymus' or Richie Repetition's it would take a forensic scientist to figure out. Her clothes are stained and torn, and her shoes are missing, so I don't notice her entrance until she slams the door behind her.

I awake to the slamming of the door and find Grace X Machina standing in a cloud of smoke from her long, skinny cigarette. The vicious early-morning sun is streaming in through the window and bouncing violently about the ribbons of smoke that have nowhere to go but up then down then up again, creating an overall effect of diagonality to the room which, to my tired eyes, already seemed a bit lopsided. I take a moment to notice this.

I take a moment to notice Grace X. Machina—much the worse for wear—and re-imagine her entrance, poetically. There's a limp that seems to come not from her feet or legs, but from her brain. A limp of broken-brain or broken-spirit. She hasn't done well for herself. She hasn't done well for me. But she has returned.

She's returned to return my gun, the gun that I borrowed from Vinnie Domino. Grace X. Machina reaches into her heavy handbag and pulls out the gun. It drops to the floor with a bang, followed by the sound of shattered glass. Clumsy, clumsy Grace.

She doesn't play it cool. She doesn't even try. She bends over, picks it up, and it drops to my desk with a bang that comes thrillingly close to killing me—I turn with it and watch it float by my face in slow motion—but doesn't shatter any glass since the glass is shattered already.

There's a crispness to the air that flows in through the window, dissolving the smoke, shedding new light on and exposing new angles of the monstrosity she's become in the few hours since our last appointment.

A banging comes from the other side of the door. Penny Dreadful checking to see if everything's okay in here.

"Is everything okay in there?" says Penny Dreadful, her voice muffled by the distance, the door, the ringing in my ears.

I've mentioned before that I don't know much about guns, but it seems like this one's due for a cleaning. There's a mixture of dried blood and dust flecked with flakes of tobacco from the bottom of Grace X. Machina's handbag caked on the handle, on the barrel, a crust of dead organic matter on the trigger.

"Everything okay in there?" says Penny Dreadful, still banging on the door.

I don't touch the gun. I look at the gun, at the way the desk calendar frames the gun. When I squint, I see a dark gun shape, off-center, against a pure white rectangle, and when I open my eyes, when I rub my tired eyes, I see the dirty details as though anew.

"Where's my money?" says Grace X. Machina as Penny Dreadful hurls herself against the unlocked door, shattering the frosted-glass window, carried by her momentum in and over like dutch-door slapstick, coming to rest on the frame, bent at the waist.

She looks up at me, then at Grace X. Machina. I've mentioned what a terrible sight Grace X. Machina is. Penny

Dreadful's scream does it more justice. Penny Dreadful screams at the sight of her friend, her source, her cause—Grace X Machina.

"What?" says Grace X. Machina, and then to me, "What's she screaming about?"

Penny Dreadful hoists herself up, still screaming, and drops back to the floor outside the door. She stands in the hallway, looking into my office at Grace X. Medusa, torso and head framed by the hole she's just made, screaming.

"What's she screaming about?" says Grace X. Machina, not playing it cool at all.

I stand and walk around the desk toward the door. Grace X. Machina shoves my shoulder with one hand, leaving a bloody, dusty print on my sleeve, by way of getting my attention, but my attention is on Penny Dreadful, whose screams are surely arousing the attention of others, if they haven't already, if the attentions of others weren't aroused even before Penny Dreadful's screams by the sounds of two gunshots and the shattering of glass.

I'm dragging Penny Dreadful across the hall to the door of her studio, when the door of her studio opens to reveal Harold Esquire, Esq.

"What is the meaning of this!" says Harold Esquire, Esq. "We're trying to report the news here, and you're causing a terrible racket."

He grabs Penny Dreadful forcefully by the arm, slingshots her into the studio, and tells her he'll take care of this before slamming the door closed.

"I'll take care of this," says Harold Esquire, Esq., and then slams the door closed, leaving us alone in the hallway.

Harold Esquire, Esq. is a good deal shorter than I am. But size is not the issue here. He's furious, a fury resulting, I suspect, not from my mistreatment of Penny Dreadful, though he does seem to be a bit sweet on her, but from my mistreatment of Penny Dreadful while Penny Dreadful is providing Harold Esquire, Esq. with free publicity, if such it may be called.

"What's going on?" says Grace X. Machina from inside my office. "Where's my money?"

"Where's her money?" says Harold Esquire, Esq. stepping toward me as I step backward into the wall.

I'm patting my pockets, looking for Grace X. Machina's quick, easy money, frantic, when I realize I don't owe her any money, quick, easy, or otherwise. She's done nothing but botch my plans since the moment she left my office, disregarding my instructions with an illegal firearm, an illegal firearm that now has two bodies on it. That I eventually wanted those bodies on it is beside the point. So by my count, not only do I not owe Grace X. Machina any money, she owes me four bullets, one window, and a legal defense. A legal defense from whom?

I don't owe her any money, I say.

Harold Esquire, Esq. doesn't believe me. My back is against the wall, but he continues walking forward until our bellies meet and his eyes stare up my nose. His breath is hot, upward-floating, carries a stink of alcohol that could mean breakfast or dinner.

"You owe her everything you owe her," says Harold Esquire, Esq. "Not a penny less."

What's a penny less than nothing? She owes me. She owes me several thousand pennies more than nothing in a one-to-one relation to the several thousand pennies less than nothing I owe her. For every bullet there is an equal and opposite.

Of course, I haven't said any of this aloud.

Zero, I say, I try to say, but it comes out like a sigh and a whisper. Zero, I owe her...

His slap doesn't hurt. I'd expected something worse, am

a bit stunned. A loud slap, and then I'm slapped, but it doesn't hurt and was less than I expected. What is a grown man to do when slapped by another grown man and the slap doesn't hurt but makes a slapping sound that echoes down the hallway like laughter? Is the laughter supposed to be his or mine? Should I stop laughing? Should I turn the other cheek?

I turn the other cheek to avoid eye contact with Grace X. Machina as she walks out into the hallway wondering where her money is.

"Where's my money?" says Grace X. Machina.

Unfortunately for slaphappy Harold Esquire, Esq., he doesn't. Turn the other cheek. He's already reaching into the breast pocket of his blazer for a business card as Grace X. Machina approaches the doorway. He has the card extended in introduction when his eyes meet hers and the screaming recommences.

Metadusa

There are muffled screams and there are screams, and slithering like smoke through the ether of these screams are the queries of Grace X. Machina concerning the nature of the screams.

"What're you screaming about?" says Grace X. Machina.

Harold Esquire, Esq.'s screams are a response and not a response both. His card seems to take an eternity to float feather-like to the floor. From the space beneath my desk, I can't see what's happening in the hallway, but I imagine I see Grace X. Machina's feet, her hands when she bends down to pick up the card, the card when she picks up the card.

The space beneath my desk is more cramped than you might imagine, a cubic space enclosed on two sides by the drawers, on one by a board whose only function is to hide my legs, but not my feet, from whoever might be facing me across the desk. On the bottom is the floor, and on top is the surface of the desk. It's a space designed for legs, not for whole bodies.

Furthermore, I'm forced to keep my toiletries in this space—soap, towel, toothbrush, razor, mirror—because it's unprofessional and unbecoming to have one's toiletries lying about one's office. Both my legs are beginning to fall asleep, or so says the tickle of pins and needles.

"Harold Esquire, Eskue," reads Grace X. Machina, "General Legal Practitioner."

Harold Esquire, Eskue's screams are becoming tiresome to me. Apparently they're beginning to grate on Grace X.

Machina too, because there's an edge in her voice when she asks him, one last time, why he's screaming at her.

"What!" says Grace X. Machina. "What!"

She's jiggling my door handle, unaware that it's locked. But just one jiggle doesn't satisfy her. No, the jiggling jiggles several moments before fading to screams. Then comes the knocking. I don't respond. I remain under my desk, rubbing my sleepy legs.

"I know you're in there," says Grace X Machina.

Her voice isn't muffled by the door since there's a hole in the door where the glass used to be. I can hear her crystal-clear, but I don't respond. She goes back to knocking, tries a few jiggles, knocks again.

"I don't want the money anymore," says Grace X. Machina, continuing to knock. "I just want to know what all the fuss is about."

Add to her knocking my knocking beneath the desk, fumbling in cramped space among my toiletries, looking for my small shaving mirror, which may shed some light on the source of the screams. The knocking stops when she sees the mirror rise above the desk beneath my hand. She doesn't know it's a mirror.

"What's that?" she says.

She jiggles the handle again and with as little success. Then she notices the hole where the window used to be, as though for the first time. She reaches into my office through the hole where the window used to be, pats around for the deadbolt, finds it, twists it, turns the doorknob and walks in.

I can see her legs, then just her ankles from beneath my desk. She's about halfway across the room when she realizes it's a mirror, and moves more quickly until I can only see her feet. There's a moment before she screams in which she examines her own face. Then she meets her own eyes and screams.

Now there's a chorus of screams spanning the width of the building. From behind Penny Dreadful's door, the muffled screams of Penny Dreadful; from the hallway, the screams of Harold Esquire, Esq., and directly above me, the bloody-throated screams of Grace X. Machina.

"Shut up!" I say to one and all. "Shut up! Shut up! Shut up!"

But they don't shut up.

"Shut up!" I scream, crawling out from under my desk, trying to stand up, falling on my face. "Shut up!" I say with my face against the floor, my own shut up muffled by my tight-pressed lips. "Shut up!" I say, on my back, massaging my legs, rubbing the feeling back into them. "Shut up! Shut up! Shut up! Shut up!.."

Clumsy Grace X. Machina shuts up, falls to the floor. And I'm left staring at the smoking gun in my hands.

POINT A

More Smells

Penny Dreadful is slightly more responsible, if slightly more stupid, than I'd previously thought—in one of those cases, my slightly was sincere—because lying on Savior Neck's doormat (a cartoonish landscape in which even the clouds are happy, with the caption, "Live well, laugh often, love much," something, I think, provided by Vinnie Domino, since there are tacky doormats before a number of the doors all up and down the hall, and since mine, which depicts dolphins frolicking in a moonlit sea with "welcome" its only linguistic effort, was there on the day I moved in) I find a large envelope, addressed in my name but with Savior Neck's room number and no postage. Penny Dreadful presumably pocketed the shipping-and-handling fee as reimbursement for the not-so-long walk down the hall.

More striking, the fact that it's dated only yesterday, the day that I finally decided to stop sending my three dollars plus shipping and handling for something I, I see now mistakenly, realized I wasn't intended to receive. Still more striking—I enter Savior Neck's room, conveniently unlocked, though I was prepared to shatter the glass, to find transcripts everywhere, years and years of yellowing transcripts, all addressed to me, some still in their envelopes, some coming unbound, stacked beneath the bed and on the little card table, atop the television and scattered across the carpet and generally littering every surface of the room, covered in dust, none of them ever read or even perused.

Most striking of all—something that prevents me from even noticing the stacks of transcripts, much less rushing randomly at one stack and reading rapidly and haphazardly first one and then another and so on of the transcripts I've despaired for so long of ever seeing—is the stink of the rotting and rotten food, the cigarette butts sticking in the bottoms of sour beer bottles, and the stench of the cat's breath, the cat who hasn't been there in days, whose gut-rot must have a half-life as long as a whole human life.

The smell causes my eyes to water, my belly to quake, to retch. It surrounds me like a fog, hovering in the doorway, intoxicating me as it slinks slowly past the threshold until I slam the door shut, hunched in the hallway, gasping gallons of relatively fresh air in croaks and gurgles.

I spit on the floor. Then I look about to see if anyone saw me spitting on the floor. The hallway is empty, and the muffled screams of Penny Dreadful and Harold Esquire, Esq., both now behind closed door in Penny Dreadful's room, amount to little more than annoying ambiance at this distance, like an alarm clock left on by an inconsiderate neighbor. My inconsiderate neighbor Fred Herring isn't around to halt the chronic beepbeepbeep of his alarm clock, and from the hallway, the muffled sound is annoying.

My breathing slows to something like its normal rate, my eyes stop watering, and the retching ends as the smell fades to memory and a tickle in my nostrils. From my hunched-over position, I squat on creaky knees and re-examine the large envelope. Except for a few wrinkles and crinkles and a small tear at one corner—all, I assume, the result of my panic—it doesn't seem to have been altered by my opening and closing the door, or by the smell behind the door.

I rip the envelope open and the transcript slips out, maybe fifteen pages, typed, held together by a staple. For a moment, I savor the weight and smell of it. There's something magical about a stack of paper that has never been read, bent at the stapled corner, absorbed in the careless way that readers absorb. The envelope falls to the floor as I fan the pages beneath my nose. I hear footfalls down the hall, boots really, a clomping as of a march, though not at march speed or in march unison. Marchers tumbling up a stairway. It's true that many, many people live behind the doors that line this hallway—nearly everyone in Discord—but none of them clomp quite so firmly or confidently. In fact, most shuffle.

I stand up, still clutching the transcript in both hands, and cock my ear toward the end of the hall where the feet are falling ever closer. Before they reach the top of the staircase, I hear the staticky-squawk of a walky-talky, and though I can't make out a single word the dispatcher says, I notice that she—it's a feminine squawk—is squawking at officers.

The officers are on the only staircase, so leaving the building is out of the question. My room is so far up the hall that the officers will be in the hallway, and therefore see me, before I make it through my own door, where the dead body of Grace X. Machina cries out for justice. Savior Neck's door, then. I take a deep breath, open it, step in, and close the door quietly behind me.

Inside Savior Neck's room, I find that there's no lock on the door, so I lean my back against it. I slide my back down the door until I'm sitting on the floor, still holding my breath—my eyes already beginning to water—as I listen to the marchers marching ever closer to the indiscernible rhythm of the squawky walky-talky.

In order to take my mind off my breath, which the smell of the room is forcing me to hold, I place the transcript on my lap and begin to read:

The Transcript That I Was Reading

Penny Dreadful: Last night on The Penny Dreadful Show, we spoke with Savior Neck, a local man, currently between jobs, who's leveled some weighty accusations against the Discord Police Department, specifically Officer Joseph Cats...

Officer Cats: There is no...

Penny Dreadful: We'll get to you in just a minute, Officer Cats...

Officer Cats: But my name is...

Penny Dreadful: Today we're joined again by Savior Neck, along with his lawyer, a regular guest on The Penny Dreadful Show, Harold Esquire, Esq., who has worked tirelessly to arouse public awareness about the various atrocities committed by men like Officer Cats in the name of the law.

Harold Esquire, Esq.: Thank you, Penny Dreadful, for the flattering and fitting introduction, and thank you for inviting us here this evening.

Penny Dreadful: Thank you for coming. As our regular viewers will remember, the Discord Police Department was too cowardly to even address Savior Neck's accusations in an open forum last night, but due to the public outcry over the whole mess, the Discord Police Department had no choice but to habeas the corpus, as Harold Esquire, Esq. might say, so we're also joined tonight by Officer Cats himself.

Officer Cats: My name isn't...

Penny Dreadful: I've already introduced you, Officer Cats. Thank you for being here. Now, Savior Neck.

Officer Cats: My name is...

Penny Dreadful: Officer Cats wants to go first. I swear, the things a reporter has to put up with to deliver first-class journalism. Savior Neck, Harold Esquire, Esq., is it all right if Officer Cats goes first?

Officer Cats: I thought you said he lived here.

The Transcript That You Are Reading

Of course, that last line wasn't a part of the transcript I've been reading but of the transcript you're reading. Officer Longarm and his partner are standing on the other side of the door, confused by the envelope they've found on the floor, addressed to my name and Savior Neck's room.

"That's what the bartender said," says his partner.

"These people get everyone's name wrong," says Officer Longarm, handing the torn envelope to the other officer. "We'll have to check this guy out too."

There's a knock on the door. It vibrates against my back.

"Mr. Neck?" says Officer Longarm, "Mr. Savior Neck?"

Another knock. He jiggles the doorknob, finds it gives, but can't get the door open because of my weight.

"He's in there," says Officer Longarm.

Together, they lean against the door, bouncing in an effort to open it. My chest is against my knees and my body's jerking double-time with their bouncing and with spasms originating from somewhere within my gut, my body's way of begging for the poisonous air.

And of course, my body is right—it needs air. I breathe, inhale deeply, an air with so little oxygen and so much else that my stomach rebels. I vomit as Officer Longarm's partner hurls himself against the door, shattering the frosted-glass window, carried by his momentum in and over like dutch-door slapstick, coming to rest on the frame, bent at the waist as shards and flakes of frosted glass rain down upon my head.

He's gasping and struggling with the door. He smells it

too. He smells the cat's breath mingling with my vomit now that the smelling half of him is in the room.

"What?" says Officer Longarm, stepping back and to the side, recipient of involuntary kicks from his partner. "What's in there?"

The last shards and flakes of frosted glass trickle down, followed by the first drops of vomit from the officer in the window. He continues his struggle while vomiting, manages to lift his weight from the door with both hands just as I jump away to avoid more splatter. Potential energy becomes kinetic. The door opens inward and to the right, leading his arms from his body until he lets go and falls to the floor, splayed and prone in a puddle of puke.

I'm standing at his head, facing Officer Longarm, who's standing at the threshold, his boots touching his partner's. Officer Longarm doesn't smell anything. At least his face doesn't indicate that he smells anything. He takes his duties so seriously he doesn't smell.

"Mr. Neck?" says Officer Longarm.

He doesn't recognize me. He was expecting an old man, a skinny old man with a wrinkled gray face and thin white hair, covered in dust and streaked with soot, like a marble statue, like the man who stole his car this morning.

"What can I do for you?" I say, doing my best Savior Neck impersonation, which isn't a very good one.

"Never mind," he says, without asking me for identification, without considering that one of us might be in the wrong room, without a sign that he suspects me of anything but being the real and actual Savior Neck, live and in the flesh.

He walks up his partner's body with a foot on either side of him, stopping at the waist. He squats down and taps his shoulder.

"You all right?" he says.

He's not all right. He's unconscious.

Officer Longarm places a paw in each of his partner's armpits and hoists him forward and upward, arching his limp back unnaturally and dragging his belly through our vomit. His partner's eyes are closed, his cheek swollen but not bleeding.

I glance around the room, embarrassed for him. Officer Longarm gets him to his feet, and throws his partner's dangling arm over his own shoulder. I rush over to the bed and clear away what Officer Longarm thinks are my belongings—my trash, my mess—and what are my transcripts, sweeping them onto the floor with both arms.

Officer Longarm half-walks, half-drags his partner there and drops him on his back carelessly if not roughly. I open a narrow door, hoping it's a closet—it is—and remove a clean-ish t-shirt. I hand it to Officer Longarm, hoping he doesn't realize that it's several sizes too small for me. He doesn't.

The silence becomes awkward, for me, not him. He doesn't seem to mind at all, doesn't seem to mind nursing his partner in the filthy bed of the wrong man. I'd meant for him to replace his partner's vomit-covered uniform shirt with my own, with Savior Neck's t-shirt. He's using it as a rag, wiping vomit off of his partner and onto the bed, onto the floor, smearing it into the fabric.

I open the only window, and the room is filled with a cool cross-breeze that battles the stagnant, foul-smelling air, alleviating some of the pressure on my olfactory nerve, but making me aware again of how very bad the odor was.

Officer Longarm finishes cleaning his partner, leaving a coat of stubborn vomit going to crust on his shirt and face and hair. He drops the t-shirt to the floor with the rest of the mess and slaps his partner lightly on both sides of the face—palm-side, back-hand, palm-side, back-hand—trying to wake him.

I search for a glass or a mug, but there isn't any, so I scavenge among the empty beer cans, picking them up one at a time, shaking them for evidence of cigarette butts, cigarette ash, stale beer. Finally I find one that seems empty, relatively clean. I take it over to the tiny porcelain sink against the wall, supported, like a water fountain in the park, by a fluted metal stem, and rinse it out several times looking for signs of grime, fill it one last time, and bring it over to Officer Longarm.

"Not while we're on duty," says Officer Longarm, waving the can away.

Is it possible that he didn't see me rinsing the can? It's becoming clear to me why Officer Longarm doesn't seem suspicious of me—the man notices nothing. He's patrolling his own little world today.

"It's water," I say, offering again.

He accepts, sips daintily from the can as though to make sure that I'm not trying to trick him into drinking beer, then, satisfied it's water, only mildly tainted, throws his head back, drains the can, and holds it out to me.

I go back to the sink, refill the can, and bring it directly to his partner. I tilt the can above his lips. Drops of water dribble down his chin. I tilt it again and his lips move, his mouth opens to accept the water. I hand the can to Officer Longarm and he continues watering his partner while I pace the room wondering how much longer it will be until they leave, wondering, furthermore, what they're doing here in the first place.

The other officer appears to be coming to. His eyes twitch and his fingers move. He lifts his arm and wipes the dribble from his chin with the back of his hand. Officer Longarm tilts the can back to upright position and guides it into his partner's hand. We sit— I'm standing, actually— in silence.

"May I ask what, exactly, you're doing here?" I say. "Besides invading my privacy and making a mess of my room."

"Your room was already a mess," says Officer Longarm.

I'm ready to deny that charge, vigorously and loudly, when I remember this isn't my room, which is always neat and orderly—even with two broken windows and a dead body stowed, with my toiletries, beneath my desk—and I'm not the man Officer Longarm thinks I am.

"I still think I deserve an explanation," I say.

"You don't deserve anything but a kick in the ass for what you did to my partner," says Officer Longarm.

I'm ready to deny that charge, too, when I realize that if this situation should take a turn for the worse, Officer Longarm could grow curious, suspicious, make a more serious effort to find out who I really am, where I live, what kind of skeletons I might have in my closet or, for lack of closet space, beneath my desk. So I deny that charge, but quietly.

"I didn't do anything to your partner," I say.

Officer Longarm looks at his partner, who has fallen asleep. He snaps his fingers near his ears, but his partner doesn't respond.

"I know that, and you know that," says Officer Longarm, quietly, then pointing at his partner, "but he doesn't know that, and," waving his index finger around in a circle above his head, as though to indicate the rest of the world, "neither does anyone else."

"Are you threatening me?" I say.

Officer Longarm glares at me as though I've missed the point. I, having understood exactly what he was saying, realize he's right. In this case it would be his word against mine, and my word isn't worth much, given that I'm newly a murderer, and the only person in town who can vouch for my character is the person who lent me the gun. I change my tone, the tone of my expression.

"I'm just pointing out," says Officer Longarm, "that you don't have any say in what I do or don't tell you."

"Will you tell me anything?" I say sincerely, even plaintively, like a good concerned citizen.

"We're just following a couple leads," says Officer Longarm.

"Is there anything I can do to help?" I say.

"No, no," says Officer Longarm. "On second thought, you might be able to help me out right here."

I'm going for eager silence.

"I'm going to leave my partner here in your bed," says Officer Longarm. "I've got more leads to follow here, and he's in no condition to come with me."

No, no, no! I need information, not a fucking roommate.

Then I realize a roommate, this roommate, might know something himself, might be able to help me out in my quest for the truth of the matter. Still, I disguise my intentions.

"Actually," I say, "I was just about to leave."

"I didn't say you had to baby-sit him," says Officer Longarm, standing up. "I'll be back in a bit," he says as he leaves.

The Real Savior Neck Nearly Forgotten

Try not to forget Savior Neck.

Longarm's Shorthand

First things first. I go through his pockets, patting him down, doing my best to avoid the now-crusty vomit on his uniform, rifling through his clothes and pulling out anything that feels like it might be of interest to me. I find a pack of cigarettes and a book of matches in the right-front pocket of his pants. In the left-front pocket, a set of keys, a few sticks of gum. In the back-right pocket of his pants I find his wallet. I remove his wallet. His license says that he, too, is Officer Longarm. I'm guessing they're related, since there aren't very many Longarms in Discord.

In the left-hand pocket of his vomit-encrusted shirt, I find what I've been looking for, what I think I've been looking for, a small wire-bound notepad, the kind you'd expect to find on a police officer, for taking notes and such. Except this officer hasn't been taking notes. He's been taking notes, but notes like this:

and this:

I leaf through the notepad from back to front, finding drawing after disgusting—both morally and artistically—drawing. At one point, near the beginning of the notepad, he'd even attempted a flipbook depicting a stabbing, though with little success, and had, after four or five frames, gone back to still scenes—poisoning a mug with gasoline, a man hanging by his neck-tie—for which he had a more vivid imagination, though as little talent.

I try to picture this man, this Officer Longarm, standing at someone's door, asking questions of a potential witness or a potential suspect, and jotting down his or her answers in a shorthand of gruesome, grisly death.

I close the notebook, feeling slightly soiled, and slip it back into his pocket. I walk over to the sink to wash, to rinse my hands, since there's no soap. As I'm wiping my hands on the back of my pants, Officer Longarm, this Officer Longarm, mumbles something from within his sleep.

"What?" I say, cocking my head toward him from across the small room.

He mumbles again, still unconscious. I walk over, trying to hear him, to decipher what he's saying, but I don't understand. I realize I'll have to ask him again.

I also realize that asking him again, prying into sleeping-official affairs from the land of the unofficial conscious, could be a dangerous thing, could be a dangerous thing with any unconscious officer, much less an officer with a pocket full of murder.

The first step in asking him again is unstrapping his holster, removing his gun, a Ruger nine millimeter—though it may as well be a blunderbuss for all I know about guns—slipping the gun into the back of my pants next to the other one, Vinnie Domino's. Then I look around the room for something made of cloth, besides the t-shirt that Officer Longarm, the other Officer Longarm, used as a vomit rag, and finding nothing on the floor any cleaner than that, walk over to the closet and remove another t-shirt. I tear the t-shirt into four strips of relatively equal size, not counting the short sleeves, and slowly, quietly, cautiously, tie his arms and legs to the corners of the metal bedframe.

"What?" I say again, sitting down on the bed beside the now harmless and still unconscious Officer Longarm, leaning in closer to hear whatever he might be mumbling.

"Who belongs to these shoes?" says the officer.

He doesn't say so much as mumble, so I assume I haven't heard him correctly, am not listening closely enough. But I've asked him to repeat himself twice now, and I assume that even the unconscious tire of endless repetition, so I move on to the next question, which follows logically and directly from the last answer.

"What shoes?" I say.

"These ones," he says, motioning with his restrained right hand as though to show me the shoes, even positioning his fingers as though holding a pair of shoes.

I don't remember either of the Officers Longarm entering my room, Savior Neck's room, with an extra pair of shoes. It is, however possible that one or the other of them did bring an extra pair of shoes, and set them down in the hallway while trying to break into my, into Savior Neck's room. I stand up quietly and walk out into the hallway, avoiding the puddle of vomit and glass, to check.

Indeed, there is a pair of shoes in the hallway, and the owner of those shoes is, was Grace X. Machina. I bend down to pick them up and get an idea of why Grace X. Machina was so clumsy—her feet would have to have been enormous to fill those shoes. Not enormous for a woman's feet but for feet in general. I suppose I didn't have time to notice, what with all the clumsiness, conspiracy, and murder.

So Officer Longarm, at least one of them, had been to the Shirley Goodness Retirement Paradise. But why had they or he not found Savior Neck there, since I'm certain he's there even now, in his father's room on the top floor of the Shirley Goodness Retirement Paradise, awaiting what? awaiting a wrecking ball?

Perhaps they'd been distracted, by a pair of shoes, one dead body, and whatever is left of another. Perhaps Savior Neck had managed to hide himself and the keys to their patrol car in one of the Shirley Goodness Retirement Paradise's many shadows. In any case, the Officers Longarm and the pair of shoes made their way back here, back to the Thirteenth Step, where it was all set in immotion, where the end is finally beginning.

"I thought you were going out," says Officer Longarm, the other Officer Longarm.

I jump. He seems to have appeared from nowhere. I didn't hear any doors close or boots fall. I didn't notice anyone else in the hallway. Of course, I was very much engrossed in the pair of shoes I was examining as he approached me, that I dropped when he said he thought I was going out.

"I am. I was. I mean, I'm back already," I say.

"Which one?" says Officer Longarm.

I'm not certain it's a rhetorical question. I stand silently with my arms dangling at my side, trying to decide whether the look on his face means that he expects an answer, or that he's finally suspicious of me or that he expects an answer because he's finally suspicious of me.

"I'm back," I say.

Officer Longarm bends down to pick up the shoes, and stands up straight.

"Forgot these," he says, indicating the shoes.

I nod, turn around, grab the doorknob.

"How's my partner?" says Officer Longarm.

I freeze, wondering how I can be expected to know any better than he does how his partner is if I've been out of the room nearly as long as he has, and am only now getting back. But he doesn't seem to be interrogating me, seems to be genuinely concerned about his partner, as though inquiring after a mutual friend.

"Sleeping like a baby," I say without turning around.

He nods, turns around himself, starts walking down the hallway, shoes in hand, then stops, turns back, walks toward me. I hear all of this, and consider stepping quickly into my, into Savior Neck's room, but then think twice. If he were to follow me in, he wouldn't be pleased with what he found. I turn to meet him.

"Would you mind," he says, holding out the shoes, "trying these on?"

He'd need only to look down at my feet to see that I don't have enough foot to fill those high heels. It's enough to make you laugh in someone's face. But I don't laugh in his face. I look at him gravely, like I'm willing to do anything to help out.

"Anything to help out," I say.

He gives me the shoes, and I slip them on over my own.

Nearly a perfect fit.

He chuckles, shakes his head from side to side, sighs, says, "I guess you're not the guy we're looking for."

"Who are you looking for?" I say.

Officer Longarm stops chuckling, looks around the hallway to see if anyone is within hearing range. There's no one around, but he whispers when he says, "We have a... situation. Somebody's been, you know," he makes the international sign for murdered, index finger swept across the neck with a twitch at the corner of the mouth. "Anyway, we suspect this guy, I thought his name was Savior Neck, but it wasn't you..."

"You can be sure of that," I say.

"Right," he says, "this guy who stole my patrol car today. Imagine that? Steal a police car to go do a, you know," the international symbol for murder again. "Anyway, we think he had an accomplice." He holds up the shoes again. "Looks like a male cross-dresser. A big male cross-dresser."

"Well," I say, "I'm sure you'll find them."

"And when we do," says Officer Longarm, making the international symbol for murder one last time before raising a hand in benediction, nodding, turning and walking up the hall.

I watch him until he stops at Penny Dreadful's door and opens it without knocking. When he opens the door, screams, unmuffled but hoarse and distant, echo in my direction. The door closes behind him.

I close my, Savior Neck's door behind me and rush quickly around the room gathering transcripts at random until I have all I can carry. As I kick the door closed behind me, I hear Officer Longarm, the other Officer Longarm, struggling in my, in Savior Neck's bed, trying to break free of it.

Tom and Dick Are Dead, Unfortunately, Harold Is Not

Downstairs in the Thirteenth Step, the screams are unmuffled since the camera is directly in front of Penny Dreadful and Harold Esquire, Esq., though they're growing hoarser by the second, the screams and the people who are screaming.

In the left-hand corner of the screen, over Penny Dreadful's shoulder, supported by an easel, a photograph, black and white, of Richie Repetition, taken before his death, taken, in fact, on the day that Harold Esquire, Esq., had gotten his case—the one involving the attack on Thomas Didymus—dismissed. Hence the fact that the patrons of the Thirteenth Step can hear the screams, are actually paying rapt attention to the screams, though none of them seems to be able to figure out why the screamers are screaming, nor why the screamers are accompanied by a photograph of Richie Repetition. The broadcast had only just begun when the screaming just began.

Enter Officer Longarm, unaware that he's on camera, standing silhouetted with his back to it, and offering, seeming to offer them a large pair of shoes, of women' shoes, high heels.

The old men of the Thirteenth Step are puzzled, and, each in his own way, worried for their collective protégé, Richie Repetition. Still, they dare not discuss their puzzlement amongst themselves, they dare not try to fit together the few pieces they do have, for fear of missing new ones, though before Officer Longarm's unexpected arrival on the set, there'd been no new pieces since the screaming began.

"Do either of you know who these belong to?" says Officer Longarm.

First Penny Dreadful and then Harold Esquire, Esq. raises an arm and points. Officer Longarm assumes they're pointing at him, but he has no idea why they're pointing at him. He glances over his shoulder, but doesn't notice the camera. When he turns back toward them, Penny Dreadful and Harold Esquire, Esq. have dropped their fingers and fallen silent, due to loss of voice rather than loss of the need to scream. Their mouths are still open wide, and if you listen closely, if you put your ear to the set, you can hear the air ejected like screams from their throats.

"Have you seen or heard anything suspicious in the last few hours?" says Officer Longarm.

Again they point, and again Officer Longarm glances over his shoulder, though the only things over his shoulder are the camera and the door.

Of course, they aren't pointing at the camera or the door, but across the hall. Actually, Harold Esquire, Esq. is pointing at the camera, ever interested in free publicity, if such it may be called, trying to get Officer Longarm to turn around and take official notice. And, I suppose Penny Dreadful is pointing at the door, if only because the door, with its unshattered window, separates them from the hallway, which separates them from my room, which is what she's pointing at. You see, Penny Dreadful and Grace X. Machina are, were, old friends.

"What are they pointing at?" says one of the old men.

"Sssshhhh!" says one of the others. "Richie's on," though it's only a photograph, taken long ago by someone farsighted enough to expect that one day, he might no longer be available for photographs, a day like today.

"What are you pointing at?" says Officer Longarm.

"Sssshhhh!" says one of the others, not realizing it was

Officer Longarm speaking with his back to the camera.

Penny Dreadful walks toward the door as Harold Esquire, Esq. walks toward the camera. Officer Longarm doesn't move. Harold Esquire, Esq. reaches his destination first , and by the time he swivels the camera on its tripod, Penny Dreadful has the door open, and is pointing, according to the camera, at something out of frame.

Officer Longarm swivels left on his bipod, and sees Penny Dreadful pointing out of frame. He swivels back right and past his starting point to find that he's been framed by Harold Esquire, Esq.

"Turn that thing off," says Officer Longarm, placing his free hand over the camera lens, and though Harold Esquire, Esq. doesn't turn that thing off, the audience in the Thirteenth Step is left in the dark, because Officer Longarm doesn't remove his hand from the lens.

You don't want to leave your audience in the dark, not in the Thirteenth Step. In the Thirteenth Step, if you stray too far from Richie Repetition, the volume on the television goes down and the volume on the jukebox goes back up and the whole crowd generally forgets what they were about and goes back to dreaming a little dream over a glass of the usual.

Savior Neck Is Not Me

Officer Longarm knocks on my, not Savior Neck's, door. He doesn't notice me watching him through the hole where the window used to be, doesn't notice that the window is broken, doesn't notice me.

"It's open," I say.

I'm sitting at my desk with a pile of dusty transcripts in front of me, one, pulled randomly from the stack, opened randomly to a page, perused randomly as I make a sort of effort to appear busy, nonchalant.

"Mr. Neck?" he says, confused to see me again so soon, in a different room. "Savior Neck?"

There used to be plenty of leg room beneath my desk, even with the toiletries, before the space beneath my desk became body room. I'm as close as I can get to the surface of the desk, and there's still about a foot between it and my torso.

"I'm afraid you have the wrong office," I say. "Check down the hall."

I'm beginning to wonder how wise it was for me to have returned to my own office in the first place, though I can think of nowhere else I might have gone to peruse the transcripts, which I haven't yet had a chance to peruse.

"I just came from down the hall," says Officer Longarm, "and so did you."

At this point, there still seems to be more confusion than suspicion on the part of Officer Longarm, which makes me wonder what it would take to make him suspicious, what it would take, once he's been made suspicious, to make him act on his suspicions. I guess a good cop is worthless without his bad.

I pull a card from my breast pocket and hold it out to him so he's forced to walk across the room to examine it. I know this brings him closer to the body. I also know that the farther he is from the body, the farther he is from the desk, the easier it would be for him to look down and see a pair of feminine feet capable of filling the shoes he's holding. He walks across the room, takes the card, sees that I'm not Savior Neck after all.

Pander/ing/ed/To/Two/Whom Etc. (Without Interruption)

Let's not delude or confuse or amuse ourselves with the idea that Harold Esquire, Esq. isn't media savvy. There are many things he isn't, including, but not limited to, a doctor, a faith healer, a good, in the sense of honest and caring, person, a good, in the sense of knowing and competent, lawyer, but media savvy isn't one of these things. Media savvy is one of the things he is.

Part of media savvy is knowing your audience. The other part of media savvy is pandering to your audience. The two facets of media savvy don't necessarily have to be employed together. In fact, many media succeed by utilizing only one or the other of these facets. There will always be audiences who want to be known but not pandered to, and audiences who want to be pandered to but not known; and without exploring whether you're pandering to the former by not pandering to them, since you're giving them what they want by not pandering to them, or whether you're demonstrating knowledge of the latter in the way you pander, we can simply say that these audiences don't exist for Harold Esquire, Esq., whose demographic is very small indeed.

Harold Esquire, Esq.'s demographic consists of the old men of the Thirteenth Step, and he knows they're no longer watching because he knows they're only interested in seeing their favorite son, Richie Repetition, whom they don't know to be dead, on the television screen.

Of course, he also knows that the television screen at the Thirteenth Step shows a shot of a bare corner of Penny Dreadful's room, from the floor, since he's placed the camera on the floor, and that someone is dreaming a little dream from within the jukebox so that the old men no longer hear the air rushing from his throat and out his open mouth, or the snip, snip, snip of scissors.

When he finishes snipping the head from the photo, snipping the eyes, the nostrils, the mouth from the head, he fastens rubber bands to Richie Repetition's ears with clear tape, and loops the rubber bands about his own ears to become Richie Repetition, still silently screaming. Then he places the camera back on its tripod and swivels the camera toward himself, knowing that downstairs in the Thirteenth Step, someone is bound to mumble, "Richie's on," and Vinnie Domino will turn up the volume on the television set while one of the other nameless old men unplugs the jukebox.

"Richie's on," someone mumbles.

A commotion runs through the bar. The jukebox is unplugged and its dreeeeooomung ceases as a gentle tide of whispered richies breaks toward the television in the corner.

Richie Repetition, that is, Harold Esquire, Esq., doesn't know how long to wait, doesn't know how long it will take them to notice that Richie Repetition is on screen, but he does have media savvy, he does know his audience, and he knows he can pander to his audience by simply sitting there in front of the camera as Richie Repetition, so he decides to err on the side of too long, since he's not averse to rolling the dice when the table's in his head.

"So you were lying?" says Officer Longarm.

He isn't so much accusing me, as asking for clarification, asking me to make it simple for him. Unfortunately, all these interruptions are making it difficult for me to do my own job, which is to boil it all down, to make it simple. It would be easier for me, for everyone, if everyone would just leave me alone with the transcripts long enough to figure out what exactly is going on.

"Excuse me?" I say.

Officer Longarm puts both hands in the air, palms facing me in a gesture of harmlessness, the heels still in one of them. He doesn't know that I know he didn't mean to sound accusatory.

"I didn't mean anything by that," says Officer Longarm. "It's just, I thought you said your name was Savior Neck."

Harold Esquire, Esq. looks at his watch through the eyeholes of his homemade Richie Repetition mask, and finds that he's been sitting in front of the camera for roughly five minutes. He decides, since he knows his audience, that five minutes is enough to more than enough time to have gotten his audience's attention, that it's time to work toward keeping that attention. He stands up, swivels the camera, lifts it from the tripod, and walks across the hall, periodically turning the camera back toward himself to remind his audience that Richie Repetition's involved.

Downstairs in the Thirteenth Step, no one has moved, no one has spoken a word in nearly five minutes. Their attention was as diligent while Richie Repetition sat in front of the camera as it is now that he's pointing it into my office through the hole in my window, back toward his face to remind them that Richie Repetition's involved, back again into my office.

I shriek. I duck under my desk and come face to face with Grace X. Machina. I shriek again, but I'm not screaming; I seem to be immune. I jump from under my desk, run over to Officer Longarm, turn him around, hide behind his back.

Officer Longarm faces Richie Repetition and his face pales as though he's seen a ghost. Downstairs in the Thirteenth Step, they don't know why his face pales as though he's seen a ghost, because they don't know that Richie Repetition would have to be a ghost to be there.

"I thought...," says Officer Longarm.

The old men lean forward en masse to find out what Officer Longarm thought. They all know Officer Longarm, but they don't know his thoughts, and not one of them has ever seen Officer Longarm's face pale as though he's seen a ghost. They don't have to ask or even glance around the room to know this about each other.

Slowly, cautiously, Officer Longarm approaches Richie Repetition. He stutters forward with a hand, the hand holding the shoes, held out before him, as though to shield himself from the ghost of Richie Repetition, as though to shield himself from further surprise.

"I thought...," says Officer Longarm.

I don't know what to do. It seems a bad idea to walk even closer to Harold Esquire, Esq.'s version of the ghost of Richie Repetition. It seems a bad idea to leave myself unprotected from the ghost in the center of the room when I have a gun. Two guns. The one I borrowed from Vinnie Domino, and the one I borrowed from Officer Longarm, the other Officer Longarm.

"I thought...," says Officer Longarm.

I pull the guns. Officer Longarm, back facing me, doesn't see me pull the guns, though I point one, his partner's, at him. Richie Repetition, whose mask is facing me, does see me pull the guns, sees me point Vinnie Domino's gun at him.

"I thought," says Officer Longarm, his eyes directly at camera level, just feet from Richie Repetition, "I thought I saw you dead."

Richie Repetition pales as though he's seen a gun. Is it possible for Richie Repetition, who is a mask cut from a photograph, to pale as though he's seen a gun? It's possible if paling comes from the eyes. Something like fear trickles from Harold Esquire, Esq.'s eyes, paling Richie Repetition's face.

He drops the camera to the ground. He stares over Officer Longarm's shoulder at the revolver pointed directly between his eyes in the full knowledge that a mask cut from a photograph is no shield, no protection from a bullet propelled at 300 meters per second from the barrel of a gun a mere meter or two away.

Officer Longarm doesn't know that Richie Repetition's staring over his shoulder, doesn't know about the guns, thinks he's the cause of Richie Repetition's paling, of the fear in his eyes. He reaches up and pulls the Richie Repetition mask from Harold Esquire, Esq.'s face as Harold Esquire, Esq. bolts across the hallway and into Penny Dreadful's room, as a soft moan, a cry for help, comes up the hallway from Savior Neck's room, as the sound of shuffling feet, of an army of invalids marching, comes up the stairs.

Savior Neck forgotten

Lost in the Shuffle

Officer Longarm steps out of the room. Looking left down the hallway, toward the moaning, he sees nothing; he looks right up the hallway, toward the shuffling, and sees nothing. He looks back at me. I hide the guns behind my back, and say nothing. He looks left again and sees nothing; looks right and sees the shufflers— the old men of the Thirteenth Step, here to see what's become of their Richie Repetition.

The old men of the Thirteenth Step, led by no one you know, and it could just as well be any of them, except Vinnie Domino, who remained to tend the empty bar, march toward Officer Longarm, shuffling, breathing heavily, some of them hacking and wheezing, but still mob enough to cause Officer Longarm some concern. Over the shuffling comes another moan.

Again, first things first. Officer Longarm knows exactly where the Richie Repetition impersonator has gone off to, and he knows exactly who the Richie Repetition impersonator is, because he was only just in Penny Dreadful's room with Harold Esquire, Esq., and even if he hadn't been, he remembers having been a guest on the *Penny Dreadful Show* only the night before, and in any case, he watched the Richie Repetition impersonator, whose name is Harold Esquire, Esq., run back across the hall to Penny Dreadful's room after dropping his camera and being unmasked.

Officer Longarm knocks on Penny Dreadful's door with his elbow since his hands are full of a pair of shoes and a Richie Repetition mask, these props being the reason he doesn't just open the door in the first place. Another moan, and the army of marchers is only a few feet away and still marching.

The moaning starts to metamorphose, sliding from pleas for help to curses on me, that is, Savior Neck, and Officer Longarm. Officer Longarm drops his props and sprints down the hall into my, that is, Savior Neck's room. He finds his partner tied to the bed, cursing just about everyone in Discord.

Now, I think, would be a good time to make myself unobtrusive if not gone. Officer Longarm might not have been able to establish the link between myself and Savior Neck, but I doubt his partner Officer Longarm will have a very tough time of it.

I put the guns back into my pants and walk over to the camera. As I stare down at it, I find to my horror that it's pointed directly at Grace X. Machina's feet, which can not only be seen from beneath my desk, but are protruding slightly. My only hopes are that the camera is out of focus, that the mob outside of my door includes all of the old men from the Thirteenth Step, that not one of them stayed downstairs, and that Vinnie Domino, who did stay downstairs to tend the bar, has been occupying himself with something other than the television screen.

There's nothing I can do about it now. If the camera has turned against me already, then the camera has turned against me. My best chance is to turn the camera against everyone else. I take it off the ground and place it on the tripod pointing diagonally out into the hallway from the left side of the door. I look quickly through the viewer to see if it's in focus and see a blurry mob of old men standing there, shuffling in place. Apparently the camera focuses automatically.

I walk over to my desk and kick Grace X. Machina's

foot, which—now that I'm consciously contrasting—dwarfs my own, under the desk, but something causes it to fall back out. I kick her other foot, and it too falls back out. I get down on my knees and use real force, both arms, to push both feet simultaneously. The feet stay in place, but I hear a thud.

I crouch low and peer under the desk to investigate, and find that, while her feet have remained beneath the desk, the rest of her body has fallen out the other side, lying on its back, the head propped against the leg of my chair, staring directly at me with its eyes open.

I walk around the desk and shove my chair out of the way. Her head hits the ground with that quiet but dense sound that always comes as a shock because it doesn't seem like it should be the sound that head makes.

I drag her whole body out from behind the desk, and lay her lengthwise parallel to it. I fold her in half, surprisingly flexible, then roughly in quarters, placing both of her arms in the crease between her belly and her thighs, and slide her sideways into the space beneath the desk, careful not to knock any of my toiletries off of the secret shelf. A perfect fit.

From the doorway, I survey my room, and find everything to be in order, in the best order that can be expected, given the circumstances. There are still small shards of glass on both sides of the room from the shattering of the windows, and if you look very closely at the floor, you might find some of the tiles to be blood-tinged due to a hasty job of mopping, but there's no time to deal with any of that just now.

The cursing down the hall has quieted, which means that Officer Longarm is untying or has untied the other Officer Longarm, and that both Officers Longarm will soon be emerging from my, from Savior Neck's room to bring the wrath of law down on Savior Neck's, on my head. And just outside my door, the shuffling in place has grown quicker, louder, and mumbling has begun to seep in through the shuffling, which means the old men are getting restless.

I leave my room, but I don't close the door, because the camera's in my room. Out in the hallway, the old men, none of whom know me, but all of whom recognize me, surround me with their shuffling old bodies, and with smells of the usual and with questions.

"Why'd you pull a gun on Officer Longarm?" someone says.

"Who cares?" says another. "I wanna know why he pulled a gun on Richie."

"Yeah," says everyone, "why'd you pull a gun on Richie?"

They've closed in on me like liquid taking the shape of its container. I swim around in them, I float, I tread. I turn in circles, glancing into the eyes of the men closest to me, and even their eyes say, "Why'd you pull a gun on Richie Repetition?" and "Where'd he go?"

These men have been dead for so long I find them hard to read. I don't know if their questions are questions or accusations, but I do know that if I answered their questions honestly, these answers would be followed by accusations, and these accusations would be true. I didn't pull the trigger, but I am responsible for the death of their protégé. How else to remind Savior Neck, how else to remind them all that they're alive?

"Gentlemen," says an Officer Longarm.

All eyes turn away from the center, from me, and toward the Officers Longarm, one of whom says, "Please return to wherever you came from or move along to wherever you are going. We don't need an audience."

Apparently they don't realize that they already have an

audience, that they've had an audience for a good while now, though it seems I'm the only audience member who's been paying attention, because I follow their order immediately. I take advantage of their order to swim ashore. The rest of them stagnate like a pond.

"Do as my partner says," says the other Officer Longarm.

I am. I'm doing as your partner says. Fortunately, neither of them can see me doing as they say because there are old men on all sides of me. They might see a slight movement in the mob, the rippling effect of me shoving old men out of my way, but they don't see me. One Officer Longarm peeks his head into my room and motions to the other, beckons him over to look for himself. They look at each other and back at the room.

"Hold it," say the Officers Longarm, but there's nothing to hold.

All the old men, save the few who filled in the gaps of my absence, are standing exactly where they were when they first received their orders, and I've broken free from them, am slinking down the hall under their cover, and creeping quietly down the stairs.

sissy face

Downstairs in the Thirteenth Step, the volume on the television set is down, and some long-forgotten singer is dreaming a little dream from somewhere within the jukebox. Vinnie Domino stands behind the bar, waiting for someone to order a drink, though the place is, to my relief, empty.

I belly up and give him a reason to live: a glass of the usual please, which I swallow in cartoon gulps. I give him another reason to live: another glass of the usual, please. As Vinnie Domino goes about his business, I watch him closely for signs of suspicion, signs of accusation, signs that he's seen something on the television screen since his customers abandoned the Thirteenth Step for a man in a Richie Repetition mask. There's nothing about the way he picks up my glass, nothing about the way he tilts the bottle and pours me a generous serving of the usual, that would indicate suspicion or accusation or anything other than a bartender serving a regular customer.

"Listen," says Vinnie Domino, sliding the drink in front of me, "I know about the..."

"I can explain," I say.

He knows about the body. He saw the feet sticking out from under the desk. He knows my name. He's the only person in town who knows my real name, and he knows there are two police officers upstairs because he's been watching the extended edition of *The Penny Dreadful Show* all along.

"I don't need an explanation," says Vinnie Domino, "because I saw on teevee. What do you need with two anyway?"

Two what? I don't have two bodies under my desk, only

Grace X. Machina, though she does have feet enough for two.

"I'd like to explain," I say. "Let me explain."

"What good's an explanation?" says Vinnie Domino. "I know you have it, so give it back."

I know he's not talking about a body. What would he do with poor Grace X. Machina now that she's dead? I suppose those eyes might still be dangerous, but to keep a dead body for its eyes would be perverse or worse.

"Give me my gun," says Vinnie Domino.

I'm so relieved I could almost cry. I almost cry, but I don't. I suspect that tears might lead to further suspicions. Instead, I reach behind my back and pull out the first gun I find, the Ruger nine millimeter—though it may as well be a blunderbuss—Officer Longarm's gun. I hand it to Vinnie Domino.

Vinnie Domino doesn't recognize it. He's seen it before, on television, seen me pointing it at Officer Longarm as I pointed the other one, his gun, at the ghost of Richie Repetition, but it isn't the Smith and Wesson snub-nosed .38—for all that I know about guns—that he leant me. It is, however, several steps up in quality and firepower from the one he lent me, so he slips the gun back into its place beneath the counter without comment.

I've only been here a few minutes, and already it's been emotionally sisyphean, so I take a moment to recuperate, a hand on my glass, and allow my eyes to wander the room, trying to keep them busy enough to merit missing contact with Vinnie Domino's which, according to my sense of paranoia, are staring at me expectantly. I'm enjoying this silence, could easily keep it up for a few minutes more, but tradition is tradition, and I see something onscreen that begs mention.

"Richie's on," I mumble, and I walk across the room according to liturgy and unplug the jukebox while Vinnie

Domino turns up the volume on the television.

So far there's very little reason to have wasted that quarter, since no one is speaking. Even the shuffling has ceased. The only sound now, and you have to pay close attention to hear it—it's easy to confuse it with the white noise from the old television itself—is the voiceless screaming of Penny Dreadful and Harold Esquire, Esq. behind Penny Dreadful's door.

On the screen, one of the Officers Longarm holds the eyeless, nostrilless, mouthless face of Richie Repetition in one hand, and Grace X. Machina's enormous heels in the other, and the old men have gathered around to examine what's left of their old friend's grandson. Finally, one of them breaks the silence.

"Who would do that to Richie?" says one of the old men, and the other old men, including Vinnie Domino, mumble grunt nod their agreement.

The other Officer Longarm, holding a sore, chafed wrist in each hand—left-right, right-left—looks up from his examination of the face with angry eyes, flared nostrils, and down-turned mouth.

"You fucking idiots," he says, "that's not Richie Repetition. It's a homemade mask cut from a picture."

He releases his wrists from his hands, releases the mask from his partner's hand, and flips it over to reveal the rubber bands taped to paper ears.

"So he's all right," the old men dare to be relieved. "He's not dead or faceless."

Officer Longarm, the Officer Longarm holding the mask, knows that he would do best to keep quiet, but he also knows where keeping quiet has gotten him this evening—unconscious face-down in a pile of vomit, bound by strips of filthy t-shirt to a filthy bed in a filthy room—and he's too angry now to keep quiet.

"No," says Officer Longarm, "he's not all right. He suffered a death last night so gruesome and painful I wouldn't wish it on my worst enemy."

I alone know that he's lying about what he would or wouldn't wish on his worst enemy, since Richie Repetition's death was no more gruesome or painful than the average drawing in his notebook.

The old men of the Thirteenth Step, both in and above the Thirteenth Step, gasp collectively. Someone swoons in the center and several of the old men in front, closest to the camera and to the Officers Longarm, stumble forward. Vinnie Domino braces himself against the bar.

Officer Longarm, the Officer Longarm holding the enormous pair of shoes, turns to his partner and glares angrily, but his partner, who knew even as he broke protocol that he was breaking protocol, who was too angry and frustrated to care that he was breaking protocol, has already turned toward his partner, is already glaring angrily at his partner when he meets his partner's angry glare.

"How'd he die?" they ask. "Who killed him? How'd he die? Who killed him?"

The questions are repeated into demands, and from demands, it isn't long before they become chants, chants of protest over the very fact of Richie Repetition's death. Officer Longarm, the one holding the shoes, breaks the angry glaredown with his partner and shakes his head wearily from side to side. The other Officer Longarm takes this as a sort of passive-aggressive I told you so, and glares even more angrily at his partner while reaching for his gun.

"Someone stole my gun!" says Officer Longarm, and, under his breath, "second one this week."

Vinnie Domino's eyes light up—I see this out of the corner of my own—and I pay even closer attention to the television screen as Vinnie Domino, trying to be subtle, pats around beneath the counter, his hand landing on his new gun, the one I returned to him, pulling it out just far enough to glance down and confirm that it is indeed his new gun, and not the one he lent me.

"Which one of you idiots stole my gun?" says Officer Longarm.

He grabs the nearest old man by the lapels, and pulls him so close that they're eye to eye with their noses nearly touching. The old man tries to talk. His mouth opens and closes, opens and closes, and there's spittle in its corners.

"All right, all right," says the other Officer Longarm, trying with his shoeless hand to pull his partner away from the probably innocent citizen he's harassing.

But the Officer Longarm harassing the probably innocent citizen doesn't let go. Instead, his arms extend to straight as he stumbles backward, stopping just short of pulling the old man forward, and remaining there with his suspect at long arm's length.

"Let him go," says his partner, swatting forcefully though not excitedly at his long arms. "How's this gonna help you find your gun?"

Reason prevails. For a moment, reason prevails. Officer Longarm lets go of the old man's lapels, his arms dropping, dangling at his sides, like a child chastened by the harsh perfections of his superior. His superior pats him on the back, supportively though condescendingly, and, unbeknownst to his superior, this adds to the child's now quiet anger. Remember, a gentle word, or in this case, gesture, does not turneth away anger.

"Okay," says Officer Longarm, the superior, "everybody line up single-file on this side of the hall."

He indicates my side of the hall. The old men stand about, shuffling again, as though they would like to follow Officer Longarm's orders, but are unable to, due to some impediment to comprehension, orientation, just plain locomotion. There's no defiance in their shuffling, but there is curiosity, queriosity, what have you.

"You heard him," says the angry Officer Longarm. "Line up." Then turning to his partner he says, in a whisper, "Why are we having them line up?"

The men, in collective fear of that Officer Longarm, and still collectively smarting from the humiliation one of their own has suffered at his big hands, obey without reply, lining up in the hallway, one by one, single file, shuffling and leaning against the wall.

"You stay out here in the hallway," says the other Officer Longarm. "Keep an eye on them, and send them in this room," he indicates my room, "one at a time. Make sure you pat them down before they come in. For your gun. For any gun, I guess."

He withdraws his gun from its holster and hands it to his partner, slips it into his partner's holster, telling him to use it only if necessary.

"Use this," says Officer Longarm, "only if necessary."

Downstairs in the Thirteenth Step, I'm getting nervous. It's my room, after all, and there's a dead body, an illegally dead body, crammed beneath the desk beside my toiletries. Worse, I won't even know if Officer Longarm comes across the body, since the camera in my room is pointing out into the hallway, where, thanks to the armed vigilance of the other Officer Longarm, I can expect precious little action, reaction, information.

As he walks into my room, Officer Longarm brushes against the camera, without noticing that he's brushing against the camera. The camera swivels on its tripod, one hundred eighty degrees, giving me a wide-angle view of my own room as it automatically comes into focus. It would also give Vinnie Domino a wide-angle view if he were watching, but in the few minutes that have gone by without a repetition, he's lost interest in the television and gone back to tending empty bar. Perhaps I'm not as media savvy as Harold Esquire, Esq. Perhaps that's not such a bad thing. If I'd been any more clever with my directorial debut, I wouldn't have gotten this accidental—I should say serendipitous—shot of all of the action. As it stands, I'm watching with something approaching giddiness as Officer Longarm takes the chair from behind my desk without any sign of having seen the dead body beneath the desk, and rolls it around front. He nods to his partner who, for fear of missing out on anything, is already keeping one eye on my room and one eye on the hallway with an ocular dexterity that approaches the reptilian.

Officer Longarm, the one in the hallway, calls the first man, the one he's just accosted, forward. He pats the man down thoroughly and a bit roughly—for this Officer Longarm, any of these men could be the one who stole his gun, and the rest are his before or after the fact accomplices by association—but finds nothing. Satisfied or not, he points the old man into my room.

In my room, Officer Longarm greets him with another nod, and gestures toward my chair with his free hand. The old man takes a seat while Officer Longarm, pacing back and forth in front of him, withdraws a small wire-bound notepad, similar-to-identical in outward appearance to that of his partner—though I'd guess, since I'm not a gambling man, that he uses a somewhat more conventional shorthand—and a ballpoint pen from his left breast pocket.

"Name," says Officer Longarm, flipping the notebook open to a clean page and uncapping the pen with his teeth.

The man tells Officer Longarm his name, last, first, middle, and Officer Longarm writes it down, conscientiously double-checking the spelling. He pulls the other chair, the one facing my desk, around the old man, and places it facing him, but he doesn't sit down. He resumes his pacing, back and forth behind his own chair relative to the old man.

"First," says Officer Longarm, "which one of you took my partner's gun?"

"Which one of who?" says the old man.

"You," says Officer Longarm, gesturing to the man, and then at the wall behind himself, indicating the old men in the hallway, "Which one of you, you and all the old men in the hallway, stole my partner's gun?"

"I don't know," says the old man. "None of us."

"Which is it?" says Officer Longarm. "You don't know, or none of you?"

The old man doesn't reply, and Officer Longarm stops pacing. He walks over to the chair, sits down, and leans forward so his face is very close to the old man's. The old man tries to formulate an answer to Officer Longarm's question. He knows the two options can't coincide, though they can and, we know, do coincide in actuality, but not as answers because if he doesn't know, then he can't say for certain that none of them took the gun, and if he can be certain that none of them took the gun, then he does know.

"Where did Savior Neck go?" says Officer Longarm, taking the old man by surprise.

Savior Neck Never Remembered In The First Place

"Savior Neck?" says the old man, taken by surprise. "What the hell kind of name is that?"

Officer Longarm stops short, performs the mental equivalent of a doubletake, considers a number of conspiracies involving Savior Neck, or me, I can't be sure anymore, and the army of shuffling old men outside the door, and proceeds to the next order of business.

"I need you to try on these shoes," says Officer Longarm.

Again the old man is taken by surprise, and again he needs a moment to reorient himself. Once he's processed Officer Longarm's request, he removes his own shoes—he's less clever than I am—and takes Grace X. Machina's from Officer Longarm without a question, though his face is asking if Officer Longarm's request is a serious one. Rhetorically. It doesn't expect an answer.

The old man crosses his right leg over his left, slips a shoe onto his right foot, and the shoe falls to the ground. He repeats the process with the other leg, foot and shoe, then looks up at Officer Longarm.

"Go back wherever you came from," says Officer Longarm. "Don't say anything to anyone on your way out," and the man goes back to wherever he came from, saying nothing to the others on his way out.

Repetition Lives

And so it goes, the same from one old man to the next. They sink slowly down the stairs, refilling the Thirteenth Step. The first old man down, the first to have been interrogated, notices that the interrogations are being broadcast on teevee. As he walks into the Thirteenth Step, he sees Vinnie Domino reaching toward the set to turn the volume down. But I'm not plugging the jukebox in, my way of protesting Vinnie Domino's adherence to the rules of order. Richie Repetition isn't onscreen; there's no indication that he'll be onscreen any time soon; Officer Longarm's questions don't pertain directly to Richie Repetition's death, therefore the volume on the television goes down, and the jukebox gets turned back up.

Alone, I couldn't argue for a suspension of the rules, but the old man doesn't plug in the jukebox either. Vinnie Domino finishes turning down the volume, then turns around to find us, myself and the old man, seated beside each other at the bar, neither of us going, or indicating any intention of going to plug in the jukebox.

We, myself, the old man, and Vinnie Domino, sit in silence. We vote in silence. The silence becomes unbearable. For myself, for the old man, for Vinnie Domino, all three, I am sure, for differing reasons, or, if the reasons happen to be the same, for coincidentally, as opposed to an absolute of human nature, the same reasons, the silence becomes unbearable, and Vinnie Domino concedes victory to us by turning up the volume on the television, and pouring us each a glass of the usual on the house.

By this time, the second interview is complete, and a second old man is on his way down the stairs as a third old man enters my room. The four of us, myself, the two old men and Vinnie Domino, watch the third interrogation sitting at or standing behind the bar, gazing upward.

To the surprise of three of us, myself, the first old man, and Vinnie Domino, the third interrogation is identical to the first. Not just the questions and answers, but even the actions and expressions of both interrogator and interrogated, virtually—I say virtually to account for minor physical differences, perhaps a bit more dust in the wrinkles of first than third—indistinguishable, third from first.

The second old man, too, claims to be surprised, claims that the third interrogation is virtually indistinguishable from the second, his own, but we, myself, the first old man, and Vinnie Domino, are not inclined to believe him. What are the odds that three consecutive interrogations could be virtually indistinguishable? It isn't until the third interrogation comes to an end, and the fourth begins as the third old man makes his way down the stairs into the Thirteenth Step, that our inclinations incline us to believe the second old man since, if first, third, and fourth are virtually indistinguishable, it becomes ever more fifth, sixth, and seventh unlikely that the second, whom I only know to greet, should be any different from the eighth, ninth, and tenth.

I lose count at seventeen, about the same time that the old men in the Thirteenth Step, at least the ones who have been here long enough to have seen a few interrogations after recovering from the initial shock of their virtual indistinguishability, begin reciting the interrogations along with the interrogator and interrogated, the relatively younger ones even impersonating their actions and expressions, to the best of their abilities, from their seats in the bar.

I begin to lose interest a few interrogations after I lose

count, and am considering moving on to something more important when the interrogations suddenly become something more important.

"There's only one left," says the Officer Longarm who's keeping one eye on the interrogations and the other on the men in the hall.

As Officer Longarm calls the last old man to him for a patdown, the second-to-last old man comes down the stairs and says there's only one left.

"There's only one left," says the second to last old man. "Fred Herring."

Fred Herring walks over to Officer Longarm and holds out his arms as Officer Longarm pats him down. Here, Fred Herring commits his first deviation from what, as evidenced by the droning recitations of the first few old men, has become the routine. Fred Herring has a gun, a Ruger nine millimeter, though you know what I know about guns.

"He has a gun," says Officer Longarm. "I think it's mine."

"Take the gun and send him in," says the other Officer Longarm.

Fred Herring enters my room followed by Officer Longarm, since there's no one left in the hallway to keep an eye on. The Officer Longarm who was already inside my room greets Fred Herring with another nod and gestures toward my chair with his free hand. Fred Herring takes a seat while Officer Longarm paces back and forth in front of him. The other Officer Longarm withdraws his notepad and a ballpoint pen from his left-breast pocket, flips the notepad open to a clean page, and uncaps the pen with his teeth.

"Name," says Officer Longarm.

"Herring, Fred," says Fred Herring, and both Officers Longarm write something down, though only one of them conscientiously double-checks the spelling.

Officer Longarm paces again, back and forth behind his chair.

"First," says Officer Longarm, "why'd you take my partner's gun?"

Downstairs in the Thirteenth Step, the old men are thrown off rhythm by the change of a few words. The droning recitation becomes a chaotic mumbling. Vinnie Domino again peeks at the gun beneath the bar, then at the television screen, where the Officer Longarm whose gun was stolen is brandishing what he thinks is his stolen gun, waving it in Fred Herring's face, then at me. His eyes land on me, they lock onto me. I can feel them on me, but I don't look away from the television.

"I didn't take your partner's gun," says Fred Herring. "I feign ignorance to anybody taking your partner's gun."

Officer Longarm hits Fred Herring in the face with a stray brandishment, though not with much force. But the old men of the Thirteenth Step don't know that. They see a gun hitting their fellow old man's face, and, without a means of measuring that force, grow increasingly angry, loud, cacophonous.

"Then how did it," that is, the gun that, strayly brandished, hit Fred Herring in the face, "get in your pants," says Officer Longarm, still brandishing.

"I put it there," says Fred Herring, calm despite the stray brandishment. "It's mine."

Officer Longarm stops brandishing and points the gun at Fred Herring's head. Fred Herring remains calm, doesn't cry out, doesn't plead for his life. He calls Officer Longarm's bluff. He thinks it's a bluff he's calling.

The other Officer Longarm shoves his partner's arms upward just as the gun goes off. It's unclear whether his partner was already pulling the trigger—that is, not bluffing—when Officer Longarm shoved his arms upward, or whether he pulled the trigger accidentally, surprised by the sudden involuntary lift of his arms. It is, after all, a small television, and I'm in no small way distracted by the cacophony surrounding me.

Fred Herring loses his calm. He creates a cacophony to call his own. He shrieks he whimpers he trembles he weeps he sweats. He crumbles beneath Officer Longarm's unidle threats. Officer Longarm grins at Officer Longarm and vice versa.

"If it's yours," says Officer Longarm, resuming the interrogation, "show us the permit."

"I left it at home," say Fred Herring, fearfully eager to cooperate.

"And where's home?" says the other Officer Longarm, still grinning at Officer Longarm.

"Next door," says Fred Herring.

Fire Hazard

Fortunately for me, Fred Herring's room stinks as badly as Savior Neck's. Rat traps are messy. Rat traps have left trapped rats behind the refrigerator, in dark cabinet corners, and in the closet beneath a collection of pretty dresses, and one of the Officers Longarm has smelled the rot of the trapped rats, and it has caused more vomiting, or so the puddle of vomit on the floor, and his pale face, would indicate.

Bad smell and vomit, though, are not my fortune. Timing is my fortune, so says the alarm clock which one of the Officers Longarm is only now bothering to turn off, good because I don't seem to have lost any, at least not any valuable time, in the course of my trip up the stairs. Cross-breezes also are my fortune, since the door and window opposite have been left open and opened respectively, in order to ventilate the room to the extent that the room can be ventilated by a cross-breeze, thus facilitating my investigation and providing me with refreshing gustlets of mellow spring air.

Still, I should make myself unobtrusive if invisible is impossible. The Officers Longarm, despite having found the man whom they think stole one Officer Longarm's gun—they remain unconvinced that Fred Herring has a permit, even as he searches frantically through the closet, throwing clothing and knick-knacks and trapped rats this way and that—continue to consider Savior Neck, whom they think is me, a suspect, suspected of something or other.

So I stand to the side of the door watching the Officers Longarm—their backs to me—standing contrapasto with thumbs in belt buckles, turning their heads occasionally toward one another and grinning at this man who they think is attempting to buy a final few moments of freedom by frantically searching for a piece of paper that doesn't exist.

Fred Herring, though, isn't searching for a piece of paper but a permit, something that would permit him to carry the gun he'd been carrying, the gun he didn't steal from either of the Officers Longarm or from any other law enforcement officials, though the guy who sold it to him—some guy who lives in the same building as Richie Repetition—claimed to have clipped it from one who'd had a bit too much holiday cheer.

He's having very little success so far. The closet is cluttered, and no matter how frantically he rummages, it doesn't seem to get any less full, as though the closet's contents are expanding to maintain a balance in volume.

The Officer Longarm whose gun was stolen goes over to the window and lights a cigarette. The other one sits down on Fred Herring's satin-sheeted bed. Fred Herring continues his rummaging, chucking another trapped rat, an empty but sprung rat trap, a slinky black dress with spaghetti straps, an enormous pair of high heels...

The list goes on, but the Officer Longarm sitting on the bed, the one who's no longer sitting on the bed but up and quietly tapping his partner's shoulder to avoid arousing the suspicions of his suspect, has fixated on the last thing listed, the enormous pair of high heels, virtually identical to the ones he's been holding for so long.

His partner turns around, sees Officer Longarm's index finger at his lips, but is unable to keep quiet when he sees what Officer Longarm's other index finger, straining to arise from the enormous pair of high heels held by its hand, is pointing at. He sees the other pair of heels; he sees the slinky black dress with spaghetti straps, and laughs so violently that he doubles over and drops his cigarette.

Fred Herring hears the laughter, and realizing that the jig is nearly up, without realizing why the jig is nearly up, begins rummaging even more frantically, so that linens and old dirty magazines fly about the room, scattering across and quickly covering the floor. A pair of boxer shorts hits the laughing Longarm in the face and he suddenly stops laughing.

When Officer Longarm suddenly stops laughing, Fred Herring suddenly stops rummaging, expecting his rummaging to be stopped anyway by official order or by a bullet in the head. He stops, still bent over, his head and arms in the closet, and awaits his fate.

"Time's up," says Officer Longarm. "Put your hands up and turn around."

But just as Officer Longarm says "Time's up," Fred Herring finds something that will permit him to carry the gun he was carrying, that he didn't steal from either of the Officers Longarm—a Smith and Wesson snub-nosed .38, though I know fuck-all about guns.

"Turn around with your hands up," says Officer Longarm.

Fred Herring begins to raise his right arm while reaching for the gun with his left. To keep from arousing suspicion, more suspicion than he's already aroused, he lifts his head to indicate slow and steady compliance. He touches the gun, fingers it blindly, grabs it and stands.

But as Fred Herring drags the hand holding the gun across the detritus of the closet, not daring to raise it until he's facing the bloodthirsty Officer Longarm, he snags it on a particular piece of detritus.

I told you! I told you, Fred Herring! Rat traps are messy! Fred Herring struggles and throbs like a trapped rat that's dropped its gun. The Officers Longarm hear the snap of the rat trap without knowing it's a rat trap. They see the gun tumble down the detritus and out of the closet between Fred Herring' legs. They see Fred Herring turn around, his face distorted by pain, using his right hand to hold up his left, which is trapped like a rat, and Officer Longarm bursts again into laughter.

The other Officer Longarm walks over to Fred Herring and kicks the gun across the room. He pries the rat trap off his hand—it leaves an angular red imprint on his flesh—and throws that too across the room. He guides Fred Herring across the room in the other direction, to his bed, and tells him to sit down.

"Sit down," says Officer Longarm.

Fred Herring sits down on the bed and looks up at Officer Longarm. He feels relatively safe as long as the other Officer Longarm is doubled-over laughing.

Officer Longarm, the one who isn't laughing, squats down and pulls the enormous loafers off Fred Herring's feet. He replaces them with the enormous pair of heels, a perfect fit. The other Officer Longarm, still laughing, turns around, sees Fred Herring wearing the enormous pair of heels on his enormous feet, and laughs even harder, until tears are streaming down his face and he gasps for air.

"Wait, wait," says Officer Longarm between gasps and guffaws, "you forgot this."

He holds up the slinky black dress with spaghetti straps.

"Let's go," says the other Officer Longarm. "We'll bring it with us."

"It may still have evidence on it," says the other Officer Longarm. "I wouldn't want to risk losing or contaminating it by carrying it around with me. He'd better wear it to the station, just to be on the safe side."

He throws the dress at Fred Herring, who, after what he's been through during the course of his interrogation, knows better than to test this Officer Longarm. He unbuttons his shirt with the intention of putting the dress on. Officer Longarm bursts into fresh laughter.

"Stop messing around," says the other Officer Longarm. "We've got to get him downtown."

Fred Herring stops unbuttoning his shirt just as Officer Longarm, the one who threw the dress at him, pulls two guns—his partner's from his holster, and Fred Herring's from his pants—and points one each at Officer Longarm and Fred Herring.

"Put it on," says the Officer Longarm with the guns.

Framed Herring

Downstairs in the Thirteenth Step, the old men have worked themselves into a frenzy. Some of them are still reciting the interrogation, mantra-style, as though it could force Fred Herring's interrogation to return to the path of least resistance, virtually indistinguishable from the broadcast for the rest of the unbroadcast. Others are dreaming a little dream from within their own little jukebox, because the jukebox hasn't been plugged back in, and the volume on the television hasn't been turned back down. Still others are sitting in stunned silence, staring at the screen on which they see only a solitary room in which there's no sound but white noise and the occasional raised voice overheard through muffling walls and traveling out open doors around corners and through shattered windows floating indecipherable upon a pleasant cross-breeze that the camera, out of boredom, registers as crackling thunder.

When I come down the stairs, all eyes turn toward me expectantly, and I see the universal disappointment in them as they recognize their nameless comrade whom none of them, save Vinnie Domino, has suspected of anything—despite having seen me pointing guns at Officer Longarm, Richie Repetition, and Harold Esquire, Esq.—such is my anonymity, even amongst acquaintances.

"Well?" says Vinnie Domino as I make my way toward him, toward the bar, the old men parting like liquid before me and closing like same after I have passed, though I arrive at the bar without a drop on me, and drink deeply from the first glass I find, which has been set there for me by the barkeep himself.

I see him looking at me for answers—or was it a confession—so I devote more attention to my glass, tipping my head back to drain every drop, putting up the index finger of my other hand, to indicate that I need a moment, but Vinnie Domino thinks I mean to indicate that I need another, so he pours me another drink.

Another chance to delay. I set down the empty glass with my head still tilted back, and lift the full one to my lips spilling streams of the usual across my cheeks and down my jowl-line. I gulp and spill and gulp until the glass is empty and my shirt is stained. Then I clock the glass on the bar and wipe my mouth with my sleeve before upping my head right and returning Vinnie Domino's gaze.

"So?" says Vinnie Domino, and the silence surrounding me turns the question into a chorus.

The problem is, I'm so exhausted. It's all just too much to go through in so short a period of time, sewing discord into the hearts of Discordants again and again, only to find that their discord is naturally occurring and as discordant as mine, then forgetting and beginning again all too soon, just as they do, if they ever manage to remember in the first place. They won't think therefore they are. As good as dead.

I concede. The spoils of Discord are already spoiled, and I'll be lucky to get out of this one with my life, which is all I wanted Savior Neck or any of them, with a few exceptions, to get out of it themselves: Surprise! It was a big joke all along. We just thought pretending you were condemned to death would be a good way of reminding you that you're alive. I never drew straws at all. I'm not a gambling man. But now I'm forced to become a gambling man in order to survive.

As I see it, my options are:

1. confess now and hope for leniency, or
2. blame it all on Fred Herring.

Confession seems the bigger risk. Between the mob of old men still devoted to their dead friend down here in the bar and the lunatic police officer who's pulled a gun on his own partner upstairs, the odds are against my walking away from this mess. There's nothing more life-affirming than risking one's life, but there's little more life-denying than death.

Blaming it all on Fred Herring wouldn't take much bluffing. The shoes fit. Anyway, he's guilty of more deaths than I am, directly or indirectly, and his own death would not likely make Discord a worse place.

"They had him try the shoes on," I say.

"And?" says Vinnie Domino.

"They fit," I say.

The sound of old men gasping is followed by the clomp-clomp of boots and the click-click of high heels. All eyes, except for mine, which don't want to be recognized by the Officers Longarm, turn toward the stairs expectantly. The gasps grow gaspier as the officers escort Fred Herring—all gussied up with some peculiar cosmetics for a night on the downtown—down, down the stairs.

"I am framed!" says Fred Herring, and Officer Longarm, still holding both guns, applies more makeup with the butt of one.

The other Officer Longarm speeds up their descent, trying to get out before his partner manages to do any more damage before a number of attentive witnesses, causing Fred Herring to stumble on his high heels. Even the Officer Longarm with the guns, realizing what he's done, speeds up a bit, and they exit without another word.

"It's true," says Vinnie Domino, having prudently waited until the door closed completely behind them. "He was framed."

I look around me, aware that looking around could

arouse some suspicions, but find that everyone else, all the other old men, is looking around too, wondering who framed Fred Herring, who knows who framed Fred Herring.

"But the shoes fit," I say.

All eyes are now on me, on myself and Vinnie Domino, the two authorities, defense and prosecution, though which of us is which remains to be seen, hinges on Vinnie Domino's response, or my response to Vinnie Domino's response.

"Fred Herring didn't make a very pretty lady," says Vinnie Domino.

Domino Falls

She's still very pretty. Despite her big feet, despite her death, Grace X. Machina is still pretty when she falls through the ceiling in a shower of sparks and flame and lands atop Vinnie Domino, pinning him to the floor, unconscious. In fact, it's a beautiful sight to see, a beautiful combination of body and fire and debris topped off by a desk, my desk, falling through a now-larger hole in the floor of my room, in the ceiling of the Thirteenth Step.

Yes, another fortuitous fire. Began in the room next door to mine, above the Thirteenth Step, Fred Herring's room, possibly formerly Fred Herring's room when you consider what could now be happening to Fred Herring at the hands of that lunatic, cigarette-dropping-into-piles-of-clothes Officer Longarm, whom, you'll remember, happened to drop a lit cigarette on the pile-of-clothes-littered floor in order to laugh at Fred Herring, the crossdressing murderer, denounced by his own fashion sense, by his own enormous feet.

Who can poeticize the way that science spreads in the form of fire? Not poets or scientists or firemen. Fire just spreads, filling upper floors with smoke, heating hallways to unbearabilities, papering walls with painful patterns, causing the voiceless to scream even louder. Harold Esquire, Esq. and Penny Dreadful are screaming even louder, have been screaming even louder, but no one hears them. Even louder than silence is still only slightly more than silence, like the white noise on the television, like the crackling of the fire that we all would have noticed on the television had we only been watching the television instead of accusing who? me? of causing whatever has recently been the topic of accusations, and no one would have believed them anyway, thanks to all of their senseless screaming. "They're screaming again," someone might have said, though really it would have been "still," if someone had cared to say.

Harold Esquire, Esq. and Penny Dreadful are trapped upstairs. We know this because one of us, one of the old men, looked up at the television screen in the commotion and saw that Richie Repetition was on television.

"Richie's on," said one of the old men.

Harold Esquire, Esq. apparently had the presence of mind to replace his face with Richie Repetition's, and is standing in front of the camera in my room miming his terror. Penny Dreadful is cautiously circling the hole in the floor—though we can't see her through the hole in the ceiling because there's so much debris—desks, bodies, flames—on the floor of the Thirteenth Step beneath the hole—and is standing at the shattered window, miming her own terror into the dark street below.

The old men aren't so stupid that Harold Esquire, Esq.'s Richie Repetition impersonation can fool them twice in one night, and they aren't so compassionate that they'd risk their own lives to save either Harold Esquire, Esq. or Penny Dreadful, not now that Richie Repetition's dead, Richie Repetition having been, for the old men of the Thirteenth Step, the only justification for the existence of either of them. They see the flames and fright and realize it would mean risking their lives to even attempt saving them, and that if they aren't risking their lives now just by sitting in the Thirteenth Step, they soon will be.

The old men race out of the Thirteenth Step, all of them except for me. I stick around to make sure that Vinnie Domino will not be pointing the finger at me, that even his finger is dead. I look down at the pile of rubble behind the bar, and can barely make out the shapes of Vinnie Domino's extremities, his feet, his hands, his head, beneath Grace X. Machina's body beneath the desk, beneath bits of floor and ceiling and insulation, beneath the occasional flame still alive but not thriving on the heap. Things are looking up for me even as I look down, certain he's out for good.

But it's better to be safe than certain. How many certainties have proven uncertainties in only a few days, in only a few hours. I grab a bottle from the bar, a large bottle of high-proof liquor, and pour my libation over the desk, the ceiling, the bodies. I leave them soaking in alcohol to mingle with the smoldery coals that mingle with the desk, the ceiling, the bodies, to await the flames which are surely on their way.

Reframed

Outside of the Thirteenth Step, night has fallen, and the flames and sparks fall, and the ashes fall, sprinkling the streets with streaks of black and gray, and the old men are sprinkled and streaked like Savior Neck before them, and Thomas Didymus before him, as the smoke rises. The scene is staticky-silent, like so much in Discord.

Penny Dreadful and Harold Esquire, Esq., still exercising futility in his Richie Repetition mask, stand in my window screaming silently louder, and the old men down below look up at them, then over at me, up at them, back at me, as they, Penny Dreadful and Harold Esquire, Esq., point down at me. Someone in the crowd, between glances at them and me, remembers that as of a few moments ago, I was poised to be either defendant or prosecutor in the case of Fred Herring vs. the possibility that Fred Herring was framed, and soon enough, others remember the same, and others still, until they've all stopped glancing back and forth between them and me and are staring at me, so that only I'm left staring at them, Penny Dreadful and Harold Esquire, Esq.

"You framed Fred Herring?" someone says, though it's possible I misheard, that my ear had its fear confirmed by rhyme.

Who/you.

"Yeah, who framed Fred Herring?" say the rest of the old men, and yet I'm unsure— though I'm sure they're saying who—that they're not saying "you," as in, "It is you who framed Fred Herring," when they say, "who." Either way, when they say "who," they're saying, "It is you who knows who framed Fred Herring."

I promise that this is the last time we won't delude or confuse or amuse ourselves into imagining that fate dropped the Richie Repetition mask into my hands. And Harold Esquire, Esq. didn't do it either, didn't do it on purpose. I just happened to be the only person still looking up at them, at Penny Dreadful and Harold Esquire, Esq., when the heat from the fire melted the bond that stuck the clear tape to the photographic paper. All other eyes, those of the old men, of Penny Dreadful, of Harold Esquire, Esq. himself, were on me until the mask slipped down from Harold Esquire, Esq.'s face and out through the shattered glass window, and even as Harold Esquire, Esq. grasped at the falling mask, he couldn't call anyone's attention away from me, because he couldn't call.

The line from point A to point B is long and twisted, and this time I force myself to keep track of it. The mask floats feathery, oblivious to Harold Esquire, Esq.'s desperate attempts to snatch it from the air below him, still convinced that it could be worth something to him, convinced that the loss of this mask is the final nail in his coffin. What he doesn't realize is that his coffin is already nailed shut because there's no coffin. Soon he'll be buried in the sky like a Scythian.

The mask doesn't drop into my hands. It floats above the head of the old man closest to me. His eyes, like those of all the other old men, are upon me, and they don't follow my eyes, which follow the mask, away from Harold Esquire, Esq. and down, down toward the old man closest to me. I pluck it from the air the instant before it would have landed on his head.

The distance between point A and point B is the distance between man and god, between the possibility where possibility is enough, of vengeance being enacted upon me, and vengeance being mine. The old men see the mask in my hand, and I am absolved, absolved in the sense in which it was meant to be meant, my sins, and the suspicion that I sin, forgiven and forgotten, indirectly saved by grace, following close on the enormous heels of indirect implication by grace. The question is no longer "You framed Fred Herring," but "Who framed Fred Herring?" and the truth is not who framed Fred Herring, but my answer:

"The same man who killed Richie Repetition. He's hiding out in his father's room on the top floor of the Shirley Goodness Retirement Paradise."

As Savior Neck is hiding out in his father's room on the top floor of the Shirley Goodness Retirement Paradise

The old men of the Thirteenth Step, which, along with my room and all of the other rooms above it, and any of the people left in the rooms above it including Harold Esquire, Esq. and Penny Dreadful, is unsalvageable, and even if it were salvageable, it would not be salvaged because some of the old men of the Thirteenth Step are retired firefighters and some of their sons are even now firefighters, are mobilizing, not to salvage the Thirteenth Step but to enact my vengeance upon Richie Repetition's murderer and upon the building, long ago unsalvaged by fire, where Richie Repetition's murderer is hiding.

As Savior Neck is hiding out in his father's room on the top floor of the Shirley Goodness Retirement Paradise and the old men are mobilizing to enact my vengeance upon Richie Repetition's murderer

The Officers Longarm are changing course. The police station is not so far from the Thirteenth Step, but the going's slow when you're walking, for lack of a patrol car, the keys for your patrol car, and escorting a man in enormous high heels, slow enough that they're still a block from the police station when they're overtaken by the strangest parade the city's ever seen—dozens of shuffling old men, some of them carrying torches, frankenstyle, others walking in shadow, bending down and picking up stones, launching them at the windows of bars and rooms above bars that line Main Street, walking alongside a fire truck, and, stranger still, a crane owned by the Discord Deconstruction Company.

As the people of Discord are awakened from sleep or stupor by glass shattering and the horn of the fire truck and the sound of heavy deconstruction machinery so late at night, they rush to windows they don't need to open because the windows are broken, and stick their heads out, compelled by curiosity and excitement to jump outside and join the parade.

One Officer Longarm, the one with two guns, likes what he sees, and adds to the noise by firing his guns into the air. The other Officer Longarm doesn't like what he sees, and grabs the nearest old man by the arm, asking him what the hell's going on.

"What the hell's going on?" says Officer Longarm.

But the old man is carried away by the current—more electric than river-like—before he has a chance to answer, and Officer Longarm is pulled in behind him, and behind him, the other Officer Longarm, still firing his guns into the air.

As Savior Neck is hiding out in his father's room on the top floor of the Shirley Goodness Retirement Paradise, and the old men are mobilizing to enact my vengeance upon Richie Repetition's murderer, and the Officers Longarm are changing course

Fred Herring, too, is changing course, in the same direction as the Officers Longarm, which is, he supposes, better than staying on course, toward the police station where God only knows what could have happened if the Officer Longarm who didn't force him to put on his slinky black dress and high heels had left him alone, even for a moment, with the Officer Longarm who did. One thousand lunatics are better than one lunatic in this case, though as he's pulled into the current, he trips over his heels, and others trip over his heels, and he's trampled until his mob mentality resurfaces, and he finds the presence of mind to remove his heels to better join the crowd, to aid the crowd in their efforts to serve up a plate of hot revenge, empty calories.

As Savior Neck is hiding out in his father's room on the top floor of the Shirley Goodness Retirement Paradise, and the old men are mobilizing to enact my vengeance upon Richie Rep ex-boss murderer, and the Officers Longarm are changing course, and Fred Herring, too, is changing course

I am not dreaming a little dream.

As Savior Neck is hiding out in his father's room on the top floor of the Shirley Goodness Retirement Paradise, and the old men are mobilizing to enact my vengeance upon Richie Repetition's murderer, and the Officers Longarm are changing course, and Fred Herring, too, is changing course, and I am not dreaming a little dream

The sun slowly climbs the sky, but I don't see it because it's on the other side of the world and I'm inside the Shirley Goodness Retirement Paradise, in the stairwell, climbing just as slowly, winded from my sprint from the Thirteenth Step, without a match to light my way, stumbling over paper, pipes, people toward my witching hour, toward Savior Neck, the top floor. I don't know what to expect, but I climb as though instinctively, toward the only place where fate can't reach me.

Pausing at the top to catch my breath, I gaze down into the darkness of staircases closing in on each other into blackness and wonder, finally, what, beyond the desire to escape fate, could have brought me here. Certainly not Joey Katz, though Joey Katz seems to be waiting for me, is seated here on the twelfth step of the thirteenth floor with an expression that seems to say "My wait is over because I've been waiting for you," unless that expression isn't really an expression. Perhaps it's an effect of the shadows of the Shirley Goodness Retirement Paradise acting upon his face that seems to give it that waiting-for-me expression, or perhaps it's the fact that he begins to speak as soon as I reach the top floor, as though he's been waiting for me, though he doesn't say he's been waiting for me. He says:

"I wouldn't drink that if I were you."

There's nothing to drink. Just me and a gun and Joey Katz.

"Joey Katz," says Joey Katz, offering his hand.

I know who he is. I don't shake his hand. I don't shake his hand because I know who he is.

"I know who you are," I say.

"You're not from around here, are you," says Joey Katz.

I'm about to tell him that he knows damn well I'm from around here when I realize he's just delivering his lines. I play along. For a moment, I'll play along.

"I was just going to say the same thing about you," I say.

"Me," says Joey Katz, surprised to the point of taking offense. "I live just up the road, in a room above a bar."

Then I stop playing along.

"No you don't," I say. "You're a squatter."

"You're shitting me," he says, again with that accusatory expression of surprise.

"No," I say, "really, you live right here in the Shirley Goodness..."

"Never heard of it," says Joey Katz.

He leans back, resting his elbows on the thirteenth step, the landing of the thirteenth floor. The surprise has left his face, leaving his intricate features to fend, unsuccessfully, for themselves.

"I was just saying," says Joey Katz, although his lips don't seem to be moving, and if they are, nothing else is, "I wouldn't drink that if I were you."

Would it be ridiculous of me to scan the stairwell absent-mindedly, looking for what Joey Katz wouldn't drink if he were me? Yes, it would be ridiculous, and I don't. There's no mug of holiday cheer. If there ever was one, it's been replaced by a gun. I point it at Joey Katz.

"Would you shoot this if you were me?" I say.

"Still, I'm just saying," says Joey Katz, "it's a good thing..."

"Shut up!" I say. "They're my lines," I say.

"It's a good thing you don't want it," he says, "'cause if you did, I'd have to strongly recommend you not drink it."

I have one bullet left. I have one minute left. I'd prefer to use my words to persuade him to stop using my words, but I will persuade him, one way or the other.

I take a deep breath, and run my hands through my hair, trying to compose myself.

"I assume you think you're making some sort of point," I say.

"Yep," says Joey Katz.

Is he starting to come around?

"It's all settled," says Joey Katz, "just as long as you don't want it later, either. Drinking it..."

"What's the point?" I say.

"Drinking it later's just as bad as drinking it now," he says.

"It's not like you were any better at reciting my lines than anyone else," I say.

"Maybe worse," he says.

Maybe worse. I would agree with him if I wouldn't just be agreeing with myself. Maybe worse? Definitely worse.

"O contrare moan frair..." he says.

"No. Not o contrare," I say, "definitely worse. Your lines got delivered. Your jobs got done, but I don't even know how many jobs you did."

"...Now you've done it!.." he says because he hasn't stopped.

"How many? How many jobs? How many employers?" I say. "I could start listing the ones I'm certain of, but what's the point? You're not going to confirm them for me.

You're just going to keep on reciting my lines, trying to teach me a lesson. But what the fuck is the lesson!"

People really don't speak like this, in full sentences, in full paragraphs. They speak like this:

"...You just carried out your own death sentence," he says, gasping.

"Shut up!" I say. "Shut up! Shut up! Shut up! Shut up!.." but he's already shut up. And I'm left staring at the smoking gun in my hand.

Once More With Feeling

The sun slowly climbs the sky, but I can't see it because it's on the other side of the world and I'm inside the Shirley Goodness Retirement Paradise, in the stairwell, climbing just as slowly, winded from my sprint from the Thirteenth Step, without a match to light my way, stumbling over paper, pipes, people toward my witching hour, toward Savior Neck, the top floor. I don't know what to expect, but I climb as though instinctively toward the only place where fate can't reach me.

Pausing at the top to catch my breath, I gaze down into the darkness of staircases closing in on each other into blackness and wonder, finally, what, beyond the desire to escape fate, could have brought me here. Of course, it isn't long before suspicion makes its way to the top of the stairs to deliver a message from delusion, confusion, and amusement—who are banned from the building—suggesting that I make the top floor of the Shirley Goodness Retirement Paradise Savior Neck's final resting place, as it was his father's before him.

So I'm surprised when they yell surprise at my entrance. They, that is, all of them, all of them who are in on it.

"SURPRISE!" they yell, and I'm surprised backward into a wall, sliding down as slowly as ever until I reach the floor.

Savior Neck is there, and so is Vinnie Domino, standing at the punch table true to type. Harold Esquire, Esq. has already had a few and is toasting me loudly and violently, saying, "It wasn't long ago a few of us realized..." Richie

Repetition is beside him, kinetic as ever, getting knocked in the head by stray gestures. Joey Katz is leaning against the wall opposite me with a glass in his hand and the cat on his shoulder, and the cat's breath still lingers in the air before it, the rancid breath that spells the word surprise now dissipating, but still the source of many humorous comments among the guests. Savior Neck's father stands ranting at the no-good son who put him in this godforsaken shithole. Thomas Didymus and Grace X. Machina, sans gun, are in the corner, lost in their own cloud of smoke. In fact, I'm not even sure those two said surprise. Then there's Penny Dreadful, documenting the whole thing with a camera.

Harold Esquire, Esq. finishes his toast and everyone agrees here here and sips or gulps their drinks—or doesn't notice there's been a toast in the case of Thomas Didymus and Grace X. Machina, or doesn't have a glass to sip from, like me—then there's a pause, the awkward silence of some who don't know what to do next and others who don't know how to go about what to do next.

It's supposed to be me. I have the gun. There are no bullets in the gun, but I have the gun. And I have nothing else, no one to take my attention away from, no one to whom common decency dictates, I should be attending. Even I lack ambition. Even I am a curious breed of character. Even Savior Neck realizes that I want nothing but to be reminded that I'm alive.

He mumbles something, but I can't make it out.

"What?" I say.

He stands up and walks over toward me without looking me in the eye.

"What did you say?" I say.

He fakes a cough into his hand and looks back at everyone else who was in on it. They return his look, but I don't know what their looks mean. Do they mean we're just as confused as you, Savior Neck, or we're just as confused as he is? Do they mean go ahead and say it?

Say what?

Say what you said.

He says what he said:

"Maybe this wrecking ball will help."

• • •

Someone, it does not matter who, but you know someone, returns home in the time-stands-stillness of the night. Someone prepares to crawl into bed with you in the time-stand-stillness of the night. The smell of withered flowers doused in gasoline has grown stronger.

Someone checks to see if someone has shit someoneself. Someone checks to see if you have shit yourself. Someone looks in the closet to see if there is shit in the closet. Someone looks in the dresser for shit.

Someone gets down on someone's hands and knees and peers beneath the bed. Someone sees nothing in the darkness. Someone reaches under the bed with one hand, cautiously, lest someone smear that hand with shit.

Someone's hand touches something, something that is not shit. Someone grasps it and pulls it out from under the bed. It smells of death, of withered flowers doused in gasoline. Someone still can't see it in the darkness.

Someone stands up. Someone stands up and gropes along the wall for the light switch.

The light wakes you. You awaken to the smell of your own death, of withered flowers doused in gasoline. Someone holds the bouquet of withered flowers that I doused in gasoline and hid beneath the bed.

"Ha, ha, ha," you say to whoever played this prank on you, to me.

You laugh. You laugh unconvincingly. You're secretly relieved that the smell of your own death is a bouquet of withered flowers doused in gasoline, and not the decay of your body. The smell of your own death is not yet the decay of your body. You've been spared your death, at least for now.

SPUYTEN DUYVIL

1881471772	**6/2/95**	DONALD BRECKENRIDGE
1881471942	**ACTS OF LEVITATION**	LAYNIE BROWNE
1881471748	**ANARCHY**	MARK SCROGGINS
1881471675	**ANGELUS BELL**	EDWARD FOSTER
188147142X	**ANSWERABLE TO NONE**	EDWARD FOSTER
1881471950	**APO/CALYPSO**	GORDON OSING
1881471799	**ARC: CLEAVAGE OF GHOSTS**	NOAM MOR
1881471667	**ARE NOT OUR LOWING HEIFERS SLEEKER THAN NIGHT-SWOLLEN MUSH ROOMS?**	NADA GORDON
0972066276	**BALKAN ROULETTE**	DRAZAN GUNJACA
1881471241	**BANKS OF HUNGER AND HARDSHIP**	J. HUNTER PATTERSON
1881471624	**BLACK LACE**	BARBARA HENNING
1881471918	**BREATHING FREE**	VYT BAKAITIS (ED.)
1881471225	**BY THE TIME YOU FINISH THIS BOOK YOU MIGHT BE DEAD**	AARON ZIMMERMAN
1881471829	**COLUMNS: TRACK 2**	NORMAN FINKELSTEIN
0972066284	**CONVICTION & SUBSEQUENT LIFE OF SAVIOR NECK**	CHRISTIAN TEBORDO
1881471934	**CONVICTIONS NET OF BRANCHES**	MICHAEL HELLER
1881471195	**CORYBANTES**	TOD THILLEMAN
1881471306	**CUNNING**	LAURA MORIARTY
1881471217	**DANCING WITH A TIGER**	ROBERT FRIEND
1881471284	**DAY BOOK OF A VIRTUAL POET**	ROBERT CREELEY
1881471330	**DESIRE NOTEBOOKS**	JOHN HIGH
1881471683	**DETECTIVE SENTENCES**	BARBARA HENNING
1881471357	**DIFFIDENCE**	JEAN HARRIS
1881471802	**DONT KILL ANYONE, I LOVE YOU**	GOJMIR POLAJNAR
1881471985	**EVIL QUEEN**	BENJAMIN PEREZ
1881471837	**FAIRY FLAG AND OTHER STORIES**	JIM SAVIO
1881471969	**FARCE**	CARMEN FIRAN
188147187X	**FLAME CHARTS**	PAUL OPPENHEIMER
1881471268	**FLICKER AT THE EDGE OF THINGS**	LEONARD SCHWARTZ
1933132027	**FORM**	MARTIN NAKELL
1881471756	**GENTLEMEN IN TURBANS, LADIES CAULS**	JOHN GALLAHER
1933132078	**GOD'S WHISPER**	DENNIS BARONE
1933132000	**GOWANUS CANAL, HANS KNUDSEN**	TOD THILLEMAN
1881471586	**IDENTITY**	BASIL KING
1881471810	**IN IT WHATS IN IT**	DAVID BARATIER
0972066233	**INCRETION**	BRIAN STRANG
0972066217	**JACKPOT**	TSIPI KELLER
1881471721	**JAZZER & THE LOITERING LADY**	GORDON OSING
1881471926	**KNOWLEDGE**	MICHAEL HELLER
193313206X	**LAST SUPPER OF THE SENSES**	DEAN KOSTOS
1881471470	**LITTLE TALES OF FAMILY AND WAR**	MARTHA KING
0972066241	**LONG FALL**	ANDREY GRITSMAN
0972066225	**LYRICAL INTERFERENCE**	NORMAN FINKELSTEIN
1933132086	**MERMAID'S PURSE**	LAYNIE BROWNE
1881471594	**MIOTTE**	RUHRBERG & YAU (EDS.)
097206625X	**MOBILITY LOUNGE**	DAVID LINCOLN
1881471322	**MOUTH OF SHADOWS**	CHARLES BORKHUIS
1881471896	**MOVING STILL**	LEONARD BRINK
1881471209	**MS**	MICHAEL MAGEE
1881471853	**NOTES OF A NUDE MODEL**	HARRIET SOHMERS ZWERLING
1881471527	**OPEN VAULT**	STEPHEN SARTARELLI
1881471977	**OUR DOGS**	SUSAN RING
1881471152	**OUR FATHER**	MICHAEL STEPHENS
0972066209	**OVER THE LIFELINE**	ADRIAN SANGEORZAN

1881471691	**POET**	BASIL KING
0972066292	**POLITICAL ECOSYSTEMS**	J.P. HARPIGNIES
1933132051	**POWERS**	NORMAN FINKELSTEIN
1881471845	**PSYCHOLOGICAL CORPORATIONS**	GARRETT KALLEBERG
1881471454	**RUNAWAY WOODS**	STEPHEN SARTARELLI
1933132035	**SAIGON & OTHER POEMS**	JACK WALTERS
1881471888	**SEE WHAT YOU THINK**	DAVID ROSENBERG
1881471640	**SPIN CYCLE**	CHRIS STROFFOLINO
1881471578	**SPIRITLAND**	NAVA RENEK
1881471705	**SPY IN AMNESIA**	JULIAN SEMILIAN
188147156X	**SUDDENLY TODAY WE CAN DREAM**	RUTHA ROSEN
1881471780	**TEDS FAVORITE SKIRT**	LEWIS WARSH
1933132043	**THINGS THAT NEVER HAPPENED**	GORDON OSING
1933132019	**THREE MOUTHS**	TOD THILLEMAN
1881471365	**TRACK**	NORMAN FINKELSTEIN
188147190X	**TRANSGENDER ORGAN GRINDER**	JULIAN SEMILIAN
1881471861	**TRANSITORY**	JANE AUGUSTINE
1881471543	**WARP SPASM**	BASIL KING
188147173X	**WATCHFULNESS**	PETER O'LEARY
1881471993	**XL POEMS**	JULIUS KALERAS
0972066268	**YOU, ME AND THE INSECTS**	BARBARA HENNING

All Spuyten Duyvil titles are in print and
available through your local bookseller via Booksense.com

Distributed to the trade by
Biblio Distribution
a division of NBN
1-800-462-6420
http://bibliodistribution.com

All Spuyten Duyvil authors may be contacted at
authors@spuytenduyvil.net

Author appearance information and background at
http://spuytenduyvil.net